ff

ANDI'S WAR

Billi Rosen

faber and faber

LONDON · BOSTON

First published in 1988
by Faber and Faber Limited
3 Queen Square London WC1N 3AU

Photoset by Parker Typesetting Service, Leicester
Printed in Great Britain by
Richard Clay Ltd Bungay Suffolk

© Billi Rosen, 1988

British Library Cataloguing in Publication Data

Rosen, Billi
Andi's war.
1. Children's stories in English, 1945—
Texts
I. Title
823'.914[J]   PZ7
ISBN 0-571-15144-2

Foreword

The Greek Civil War began in earnest in May 1946 and ended three years later, in October 1949. The country was split between the Monarchists (supporters of the King), who were the ruling party, and the Communists. During the Second World War they sank their differences and fought side by side against the Germans and Italians. But once the foreign enemy had been driven out Greece went to war with itself.

Things got off to a good start for the communist partisans. The majority, at least to begin with, belonged to the large ELLAS party and the smaller but fanatical KKE. The outcome of the war might have been very different for them and for Greece had they agreed to fight together under the same ideological umbrella, but instead the parties sub-divided into an undisciplined array of political units, each set on doing things their way. So they ended up fighting one another rather than concentrating on beating the enemy. The government army soon got wind of the divisions amongst the 'red camps' and lost no time in using the situation to their own advantage. They asked for help from both Britain and America, and they received it in the form of weapons and 'advisers'. Neither of those countries wanted a communist or even remotely socialist Greece.

Well, in time the 'red rabble' was defeated, and nine years of bloodshed came to an end. At last the guns were silent, and slowly the hills, where so many atrocities had been committed by both sides in the names of Freedom and Truth, lost the menacing atmosphere that had hung over them for so long. Once again people could go about their daily business without always having to look over their shoulders.

I must add that although peace had come it held, for some, one last bitter twist to it: thousands of partisans, afraid or simply unwilling to return to their homes for ideological reasons, made for the communist countries north of Greece – mostly Yugoslavia and Bulgaria. On their retreat through Greek Macedonia (Northern Greece) they carried off, by force, the children of the villages through which they passed. It was like the Pied Piper of Hamelin, only this was for real. Those children never saw their homes or their families again.

Now, in 1987, Greece is at peace with itself. It has a democratic (Socialist) government which came to power in 1980, and there is freedom of speech and political freedom for all. Thanks to tourism, Greece has become prosperous to a degree unimaginable even twenty years ago. These days all children sit down to three square meals a day, and wear shoes every day of the week.

Me, I look at the hills and keep my fingers crossed.

Billi Rosen
Corfu, September 1987

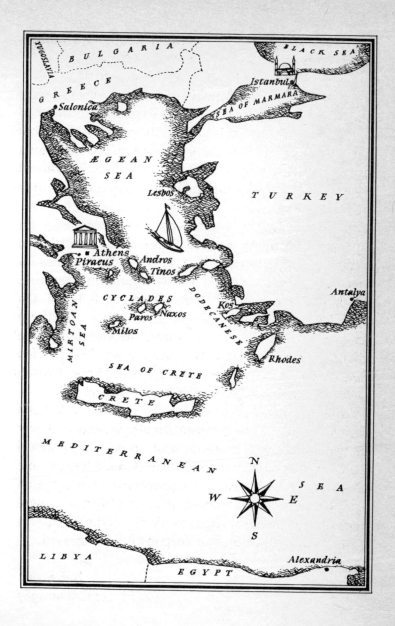

Chapter One

'And so,' Grandmother concluded, 'the Sultan sentenced Ailan the court dancer to death because she would not betray the hideout of Mahmet the Rebel and his band of fighters.

'The evening before the execution, the Sultan went to Ailan's cell to pay her a last call. "My heart is heavy," he said. "Sentencing you to death has made me feel like a murderer." Ailan, full of pity for him, replied, "My Lord, we all carry the seed of our own destiny within ourselves."

'It was not the reply the Sultan had expected and he became very angry. "Obstinate girl," he cried, "I had but one straw to offer you and you threw it away. Well, die then, if living means so little to you."

'Ailan was hardly listening. Her eyes were on a patch of star-studded sky which was just visible through the narrow window of her cell.

' "Everything that dies is born again, my lord," she said calmly, "and should you chance to look into the sky some starry night and see a star brighter than the rest, that seems to turn and leap and pirouette, you'll know it is I." And those were her very last words.'

'So she didn't live well and we still better?'

'No, not in this story.'

'And she didn't get a dress which was as the sky with all its stars?'

'I'm afraid not.'

'Nor one spun from the golden rays of the sun?'

'No.'

I swallowed hard. 'I don't like that story,' I said, my voice thick with tears.

Grandmother pulled the sheet up around me and bent down to kiss me goodnight but I turned away. 'Andi,' she pleaded, 'all stories can't end happily. Besides, it was you who insisted on a different kind of story tonight, wasn't it?'

That put me in a foul mood as well as a contradictory one. 'Well, I didn't mean that kind of story,' I shouted rudely, 'and anyway you didn't have to make her die. You did that on purpose.'

'My dove,' Grandmother replied patiently, her face close to mine, 'Ailan didn't want to die but neither did she want life at any price. In a difficult situation we all of us have the ability to choose what kind of life we want and on what terms. And how do you think Ailan would have lived, even supposing that the Sultan had given her a full pardon and let her stay on at the palace, when for the rest of her life she would always be nothing but a traitor?'

'But wasn't she afraid when the Sultan told her that she would die?'

'I expect so. After all, no one wants to die, especially not someone as young and full of life as Ailan was.'

'Couldn't she just have made up a place?'

'Impossible. You see, the Sultan knew that Ailan had been seeing Mahmet, the leader of the attempted rebellion. The question was whether the fear of death would be strong enough to make her turn traitor.'

'But it didn't.'

'It didn't because she made herself overcome that fear.'

'That was very brave of her, wasn't it, Grandmother?'

'Yes, my dove, it was. But, you know, someone once said that the only thing we have to fear is fear itself. For instance, when your mother brought you here after you were born and asked me to look after you, you were just one week old and weak as a kitten, a poor runt that no one expected would live beyond the first month or so. I took you, of course, but little did I know what I was taking on. You were a hard one to keep alive. For nights on end I didn't dare to close an eye, lest you should stop breathing when I wasn't looking. Well, one day it almost happened. You caught a chill and just lay there, still and pale. Your body was ravaged by fever – the minute lungs gasping for air, the tiny heart fluttering like a frightened bird under the transparent skin.

'I almost lost my reason that day, and fear did get the better of me then. I simply lost the ability to put two straight thoughts together. All I could think of was that I must get a priest before it was too late. And so I set off, running through the village like a madwoman, my hair all over the place and forgetting even to tie a scarf around my head. Well, I found the priest and when we got back to the house, he took one look at you and got to work straightaway. You see, he was as convinced as I was that the sheer thread that bound you to life was about to snap.

'And it was then, while he was anointing you with the Holy Oil, that the miracle happened. Who knows, perhaps the oil was too cold, or the priest's hands too rough, but suddenly you began to cry louder than you'd ever cried before and that broke the spell. It brought me to my senses and sent Death scurrying back to his dark garden. I saw then how afraid I had been and how fear had turned me into a quivering blob of jelly. Now, I decided to meet it head on, to face it and spit in its eye. And I did. From then on, things got better for us. You were ill for a long time but I didn't lose my nerve again. I didn't let fear get its hands round my throat a second time. Do you understand what I'm trying to tell you, my dove?'

I nodded. 'I think so, Grandmother.' She took a handkerchief out of her apron pocket and I blew into it and felt good again. 'What happened next?'

She laughed. 'Well, we survived, you and I, and here we are. And now it is you who must learn to take fear by the tail and bring your foot down on it whenever it rears its ugly head at you.'

'Is that what Ailan did?'

'That's right, my precious. That's just how it was.'

Now I was sleepy and content to lie back in bed and let Grandmother go. Later, when she'd given Aunt Hercules a hand with cousin Aki – he'd got so big it needed the two of them to carry him to bed – she'd come back. Careful not to wake me she'd creep in

4

beside me and I, who would not be asleep, would throw my arm across her broad back and only then would I close my eyes, safe at last from the night and the sounds of war filtering down from the brooding, thyme-covered hills that surround our village.

Chapter Two

The next day I went to meet the boat that was bringing my brother Paul back from Athens. He'd gone there to take fruit and vegetables to our Aunt Dina and her family.

Aunt Dina was married to an army captain and they had four boys. Grandmother was always nagging her to come and stay with us in the village, at least until this new war too should end, but Aunt Dina always replied that a wife's place was with her husband. I heard Grandmother tell Aunt Hercules that the real reason why Aunt Dina wouldn't leave Athens was that Uncle Tasso was a devil in uniform and she had a job keeping him on the straight and narrow. That's why she wouldn't leave him by himself. So she stayed on in Athens where there was a shortage of almost everything. Of course, as the wife of an officer Aunt Dina and her family were better off than many other people, but when it came to fruit and vegetables it was not easy. Which is why Paul had to visit them once in a while. I missed him terribly while he was away. Grandmother said I became broody and difficult to have to do with, but I couldn't help it. He was part of me, like an arm or a leg.

Still, Paul's jaunts to Athens had their good points, too. He never returned empty-handed from Aunt Dina's. Uncle Tasso, her husband, always managed to send something back for us. It might be chewing gum, boiled sweets or chocolate – or all three. I don't know where he got them from. Once I asked Aunt Hercules how it was that Uncle Tasso could get hold of so much candy when there wasn't a single fruitdrop to be had in the whole village, but she only snorted and said that the army took care of its own. In a voice I'd not heard before, she said she sometimes wondered whether we weren't on the wrong side. Grandmother had thrown her a long hard look. 'Daughter,' she'd snapped, 'talk nonsense if you must just as long as you don't forget which side you are on.'

Aunt Hercules had not said anything else after that, but it had set me thinking. The big war was over.* The Germans and the Italians had gone home and so had our friends, the English, who'd helped to rid us of them, and here we were working up for yet another war, one that had begun in the mountains but was coming closer to our village every day. Our mother and father, Paul's and mine, had both been in that other war, the one against the Germans and the Italians, but no sooner had they come back from that one than it was time for new farewells. It seemed to Paul and me that we had spent most of our lives saying goodbye to our parents.

I don't know how it was, but thinking about my

___
*The Second World War.

mother and father also made me think of Uncle Tasso. He sent us sweets, stuffed us with good food and fed us expensive pastries at the Café Rosita when we went to see him and his family, and yet we were under strict orders from both Grandmother and Aunt Hercules not to be too friendly with him. Above all we were not to answer any questions, however innocent they might seem, about our parents. That's why we always played at being really dumb whenever he was around. Once I heard him tell Aunt Dina that Cassie's children had the minds of village idiots. I liked him even less after that. I had seen behind his smile and it was a side I didn't care for.

While I was thinking all this the pilot boat had moved out into the deep channel in the middle of the bay to wait for the steamer. The little boat was piled high with crates of grapes and peaches and cherries all bound for Athens. It seemed strange that there should be a shortage of them in Athens when so much of it was going there. Where did it go? What happened to it after it had been unloaded in Piraeus?

The steamer was late, and I was about to ask Mattis the boatman how much longer he thought it would be when suddenly there she was, turning the corner by the lighthouse as gracefully as a swan. Her passengers, crowding the prow, began to wave as soon as they were in the bay, straining their eyes to see what pilot boats had left the quay, whether anyone was coming out to meet them and who the rowers were. It made no difference how often one had made the journey. Gliding in through the narrow passage into our horseshoe-shaped bay, and seeing the village that looked as though it had been built right on the water, the hills covered by thyme and olive trees, pine and oleander, travellers coming for the first time say that they have never seen anything so pretty. The houses are either pink or white or blue, with jasmine covering the walls, their courtyards shaded by canopies of vine, and the gardens are planted with everything from orange trees to pomegranates and figs. They go down as far as the sea, where the eucalyptus trees trail their slim pointed leaves in the clear water like sheer green veils.

The travellers stare at our white and blue village, eating it with their eyes, point at the turquoise dome of the church, almost knock themselves out by pushing their faces into the lemon and orange blossoms and gape at the majestic mountain, the 'Sleeper', her head thrown right back like someone laughing at a hilarious private joke, her high forehead, clean as a whistle, her closed lids resting on rounded, thyme-covered cheeks, straight nose and stern mouth, her raised shoulders, arched back and drawn-up knees. Grandmother says that she is one of nature's wonders and the guardian of our village. In the mornings she is usually draped by thick haze, invisible except for the drawn-up knees. Some like her best that way, when she plays hard to get behind the curtain of milky-white cloud. But I like her best in the evenings, at sunset, when she is at rest without shadows, her face silhouetted against the orange sky.

I'd seen the Sleeper all my life but I never got bored with looking at her, trying to guess at her dreams. I had

9

never told that to anyone. Not even to my brother or Marco. Her dreams were safe with me. And somehow, right then, I remembered Ailan and how she had died with her secret, and now it felt both right and true. I understood then that just as there are many kinds of life, there is also more than one kind of death.

When the boat came to a standstill and the cargo of fruit had been transferred from the pilot boat to the decks of *The Orange Sun*, Paul, first in line of the disembarking passengers, climbed down the side of the steamer and into Matti's boat. We hugged each other briefly and sat down close to one another. He was ten years old and kissing embarrassed him. But he was home again and that was what mattered. There were only three more passengers to disembark from *The Orange Sun* that morning: Old Olga, supported by her daughter Maro, and 'Old Cyclops', our new Chief of Police, liked by some but feared and hated by most. There. Sides again. He was new to us, this policeman, a stranger who'd come to the village about six months ago, yet already people knew which side of him they wanted to be on. Me, I couldn't help feeling that to be on the wrong side of that one was no recipe for an easy life.

When we got home Grandmother and Aunt Hercules wanted to know all about Paul's stay in Athens and whether Aunt Dina had perhaps changed her mind and would come to stay with us after all.

'It's no good, Grandmother,' Paul answered impatiently. 'Aunt Dina is not going to come now or ever. She says to tell you that while Uncle Tasso remains stationed in Athens she's staying with him.'

Grandmother sighed. 'It's the children I am thinking of. The city is no place for them, the way things are going. Their father's uniform won't protect them for ever.'

'Mother!' The exclamation had come from Aunt Hercules. To reinforce it she put a finger to her lips. It killed what might have been an interesting conversation stone dead. The place turned as quiet as a grave. 'Small pots have big ears,' our aunt added as a kind of follow-up to the finger-to-lips-routine.

Paul and I turned our eyes towards the ceiling. Grown-ups . . . But we kept quiet and instead got what we could out of the silence.

Chapter Three

Soon after Paul had come back from Athens, Marko –
who was Aunt Hercules' youngest son and our constant
companion – Paul and I were asked to go to the *stani*,
the sheep fold, with a message and some things for
Stammo, the shepherd. In return he'd give us some *feta*,
the white crumbly cheese made out of ewe's milk, to
bring back.

Old Stammo lived alone. His wife Aspasia was dead.
After her death, people thought that he would go to live
in the village with one of his many children but he
surprised everyone by saying that he was too old to
move house and would stay on up at the *stani* with his
sheep and his dog. It was a long way to the *stani* and he
rarely had visitors except for us, and we only went
because we had to. The things we took him were always
the same: olives, some oil, a small loaf of Grandmother's home-made bread and a bottle of wine all
wrapped in an old faded tablecloth. Normally we'd be
out playing in the yard while Grandmother prepared
the bundle for old Stammo, but this time we stayed in
the room with her because she and Aunt Hercules had
not yet got round to carrying poor cousin Aki to his

daybed outside and we thought we'd amuse him until she was ready.

Grandmother had her back to us but we could see the movement of her arms as she brought the four corners of the cloth together into a tight knot. Shifting myself a little, I could see the bundle before her and noticed that the bottle of oil was without a stopper. I was about to tell Grandmother that she had forgotten to put the cork in when she opened her hand and dropped something into the oil. I caught my breath. She had been quick but not quick enough. I nudged the boys and by silent gestures I made them understand what I had seen.

Grandmother must have sensed that something was going on behind her back because she suddenly turned and stared at us. 'Oh,' she exclaimed in a tone which clearly showed that she'd been miles away, 'you're still here, then.' The sun was on her face, and I could see the golden flecks in her eyes and the pupils, black as olives, drawn to tiny pinheads against the light. She opened her mouth to say something else but then thought better of it. Instead she held out the finished bundle to me. I took it, trying not to look at the bottle containing the oil. She kissed us all in turn, Aki too, though he wasn't going anywhere, made the sign of the Cross over us and pushed us out of the door.

We were already by the gate when she called out: 'Tell Stammo that to speak of the song is to see the bird.' We stared first at her and then at one another. She'd never done anything like that before. 'Repeat it.' It was an order and we obeyed automatically. 'Right,' she said briskly, 'now off you go and look out for snakes and

13

wild dogs.' 'And wolves,' we teased her. She didn't laugh. 'Well, yes,' she replied seriously, 'one can't be too careful. There are plenty of beasts about this time of the year.' Of course, there were snakes and foxes and packs of wild dogs in the hills and maybe wolves, too, but I don't know that it was that kind of beast she was thinking of.

We took the path that ran behind The Secret Corner, a taverna owned by that old grouch Ghika and his bad-tempered old woman, Loppi, who, we were sure, was really a witch. The path to the *stani* was steep and ran through shrub, lentisk* bushes, thyme, pine and oleander. Further up we left it and followed a dried-up river bed, playing hide-and-seek in and out of the giant plane trees that bordered its banks. Hours later we arrived at the *stani*. Old Stammo greeted us as if he was really glad to see us, and asked us into his hut. It was a low stone building with a corrugated iron roof, a rickety wooden door, windows without either panes or curtains, a fireplace in the middle of the floor with a black pot hanging over it, an old iron bed piled high with coarse-woven woollen blankets in bright colours. His wife's loom stood as she had left it when she died, even down to the blanket she'd been working on which was still stretched on its frame. Then there were some pots and pans hanging from nails hammered into the walls, a couple of glasses perched dangerously on a makeshift shelf, and at the far end of the room stood the barrels holding the cheese. The whole place smelled of sour milk.

*A type of broom.

I handed Stammo the bundle and delivered the message, and then we went outside to sit against the sun-warmed walls of his hut while he pushed cheese and onion and hunks of bread at us. We were dying to ask him about whatever lay at the bottom of the bottle of oil, but we didn't. We told ourselves that if Grandmother had wanted us to know she would have told us. After we'd eaten, we gave the old shepherd news of his family and some general village gossip, then the four of us fell silent, gazing at the magnificent view of the bay below, picking out the islets dotted about on the purple waters like so many pearls.

First there was the tiny Rock of the Cross with its small chapel, then the island fortress of Bourzi, and further away still the huge rock that looked like a lion, complete with head and mane, outstretched paws and raised flanks. No wonder, I thought, that old Stammo had chosen to stay on up here with his sheep and his dog Zak, whom he loved and who loved him. Zak had barked at us as we'd neared the hut but now he lay at his master's feet, asleep – yet not missing a thing. If ever anyone got it into their head to harm the old shepherd, they'd have to get past Zak first.

Normally we would have gone straight home after leaving the *stani* but we had eaten too much and it made us sleepy. We were about halfway home when we decided that we just had to have a nap before going on. But first a quick check for snakes. We hadn't come across any so far but that didn't mean that there weren't any. We began to beat a patch of ground in the shade of the old plane trees, but instead of making us even more tired it gave us a second wind and we went on beating and kicking at the shrubs and bushes just for the fun of it, running at them like an army on attack, crashing into one another and falling headlong into a prickly hedge growing up against a high rock.

Falling into that hedge was like falling into a pin-cushion. I would have cried from the pain of it had the boys not been there. They probably felt the same, about not letting on how much it hurt, I mean, so we gave vent to our pain by yelling out things that would have had Grandmother rushing for the soap if she had been there to hear us. We were hopping around like savages, shouting and licking the bloody scratches on our arms and legs, when Marko suddenly fell to his knees and began to crawl through a gap in the hedge.

Paul put his finger to the side of his head and rotated it anti-clockwise. 'Found something to eat then, have we?' he teased, as Marko's plump body disappeared through the hole. Marko never passed up anything that could be sucked, chewed or swallowed.

'Shut your face, cretin,' came Marko's voice from the other side of the hedge. 'I think I've found something.'

'What?' Paul and I shouted together.

'Get down here,' was the muffled reply.

'Best to humour the lunatic,' Paul whispered and then he and I, too, got down on our knees. It was awful getting through that hedge. When we at last came out on the other side we looked as if we'd been fighting tigers and lions. But our efforts were rewarded. In front of us, close to the base of the rock, was another opening. Still on all fours we filed through it, heedless of what might lie on the other side. It was very cold and very dark inside the cave. Not having any idea of its height, we rose slowly and were pleased to find that we could stand upright with room to spare.

In the narrow band of grey light that poured in through the low opening we began to take stock of our discovery. The floor was hard and smooth, the walls uneven with sharp rocks sticking out of them, the ceiling as high as the dome of a church. To begin with, that was all we saw but as our eyes became more accustomed to the gloom we picked out an old tin, a *brikki*,* and a small rusted spoon. At the very far end of the cave we stumbled over a long thin wooden box, a bit like a coffin but not quite. I ran my hands over it and around it and felt the padlock. A locked box that looks like a coffin but isn't ... Well, one only locks things away that are either very precious – or that one wants to keep a secret. It wasn't necessary to put two and two together to realize that others had been to the cave before us. Others, with secrets and things to hide.

'Paul, Marko,' I whispered, suddenly afraid of my own voice.

'What?' Paul whispered back.

'I think we should go now.'

'I'd like to know what's in that box, first.'

'Not a chance,' broke in Marko, 'not without a crowbar or something like that.'

'Won't the spade do?'

'No way.'

---

*A small, long-handled pan for making Greek/Turkish coffee.

17

'Well, then let's bash it with a rock.'

'Don't be daft. This isn't the sort of lock one uses for hen-houses, you know. You feel the size of it.'

Marko was right. It was a big, heavy lock, the kind used to lock up shops and warehouses. It would take more than just a stone to crack it open.

'We'll have to come back, that's all,' Marko said, as if getting up here was the easiest thing in the world. Still, if we wanted to find out what was in that box, a return trip with the right tools was the only answer.

We crawled out of the cave and through the hedge, collecting more scratches and tears as we went. Before we left the scene, we mended the gap in the hedge as best we could by piling dead branches and other wood in front of it. Then we set off for the village, tumbling down those hills as if the Devil was at our heels.

Chapter Four

Two weeks passed before we could return to the cave. We'd waited, hoping for another trip to the *stani* which would give us the perfect excuse we needed to be in the hills all day, but the days passed and Grandmother did not seem in a hurry to send any more messages to the old shepherd. The first opportunity we had was when, one morning at school, the teacher announced that there would be no lessons for the next couple of days as he had to attend a teachers' conference in Athens.

Knowing that Grandmother and Aunt Hercules were bound to draw up lists of jobs for us to do if they got to know of our holiday, we 'forgot' to tell them of it. But we weren't all bad. We did take the pitchers to the village to fill them before we went. Mumbling something about having to hurry or we'd be late for school, we gave The Secret Corner a wide berth this time (grouchy Ghika was bound to tell on us if he saw us). Instead we took the path through Notta the Herb-picker's little lemon grove on the outskirts of the village.

Two hours later we were at the cave. Making sure no one was about – the risk of being spotted by a goatherd was real enough – we braced ourselves for the haul through the wall of thorns. At the mouth of the cave I switched on the torch that I had brought. Drawing courage from the slim beam of light, we went inside and noticed at once that things had changed.

Last time there had been only one box, now there were at least fifty, stacked one on top of the other as neatly as coffins at an undertaker's. 'Holy Archangel,' whispered Paul. 'That naughty box has gone and had babies,' Marko howled. We giggled but more because of a sudden attack of nerves than because we found it funny. The tension in the cave had become unbearable, making the hair at the back of our necks stand up stiff and straight like the bristles on a hog's back. Our instinct told us to get out – now. Cover up the hole in the hedge and forget what we'd seen. Only, how could we?

Having come so far, it was impossible to leave without a peep into those boxes. We all helped to heave the iron bar that we'd carried up with us into the side of one of the boxes. It took a while to make a hole big enough to allow us to see inside, but we didn't give up until we had done it. A hole the size of a plate was all that was needed. The torch did the rest.

I don't know what we'd expected to find. What we did find was arms. Crate upon crate of rifles. The war was making its way down the hills like some unstoppable disease.

'Dear God,' I exclaimed.

'Sweet Jesus,' whispered Paul.

'Holy Maria,' whistled Marko.

It was perhaps not the most polite way of addressing the Holy Family, but we just had to tell someone.

Chapter Five

After that, things went from good to bad and from bad to worse. That's what I thought anyway. Suddenly there began to be fights in the tavernas and in the dark alleyways between the houses and between men who had never fought one another before. Neighbours stopped speaking to one another, families who'd been friends were suddenly enemies. Husbands, fathers, sons, staggered home wounded, bleeding from cuts that could only have been made by knives. Some lost ears, others were left with angry scars across their faces, while a few were so badly cut up they had to be taken to the hospital in Athens. Grandmother said that the men used knives because they were quick and silent and easy to hide. Used right, there was next to no pain, as every good butcher knew.

Grandmother knew what she was talking about. She did all the slaughtering at home. She didn't like it but there was no one else to do it. We were too young to help with something like that and as for Aunt Hercules, she was useless. At the first sight of blood she'd begin to moan as if it was her head that was on the block and then she'd faint. So it was left to Grandmother to 'tickle' the necks of the chickens and turkeys and rabbits that had been marked for the pot.

Once we were given a pig but it soon became clear that we would not be able to keep it. There simply weren't enough left-overs for it to eat. So Grandmother decided that if we couldn't feed it, it might as well feed us. She had never slaughtered anything so big. She knew her way about the necks of rabbits, chickens and turkeys, but the neck of a pig was unknown territory to her. In short, she made a mess of it. Every time she plunged the point of the knife into its neck it would leap into the air, crazy with fear, the blood gushing from the various wounds in thin jets colouring them both crimson. I'd never seen Grandmother cry but I did then. Tears, mixed with the blood from the pig, streamed down her face like the waters from a burst dam. In the end the pig did die, but I think it did so from exhaustion rather than because Grandmother had managed to find the right artery. We had no scruples about eating that unlucky pig. Roast pork was Christmas and Easter and one's Name Day rolled into one. Only Grandmother did not let any of it pass her lips.

We never had another pig. After it had all been eaten up, it was back to chickens and rabbits and turkeys, and once a year, at Easter, kid. But mostly it was chickens. They were the easiest of all to kill. Chickens, I must tell you about them. It was like this. We had some chickens that caught some illness and died. Chickens are useful animals to have, so, of course, we bought a new batch. We got these from our neighbour Ritzo. He was supposed to have a particularly healthy breed and that's why we bought them from him and not from the gypsies who travelled the country selling chickens and turkeys. So, a lot was expected of Ritzo's chickens. After all, they had a reputation to live up to.

But day after day passed and there were no eggs. Ritzo's chickens refused to lay. Grandmother said that perhaps one had to give them time to settle in but after two weeks, when there were still no more than a handful of eggs, Grandmother grabbed a hen, tucked it under her arm, ordered us to drop whatever we were doing and fall in behind her. We did. Instantly. One look at Grandmother's face told us that something exciting was about to happen.

We advanced on Ritzo's house like a raiding party with Grandmother at the head, then me (I was the oldest), then Paul, and last in line, Marko. Grandmother would have made Aunt Hercules follow with Aki had he not been so big or so heavy to carry. We drew up in front of Ritzo's gate and held our breath while Grandmother pounded it with her fist. Moments later it was thrown open by an astonished Ritzo.

'I was sure it was the Germans all over again,' he said jokingly. Then his eye caught sight of the bird under Grandmother's arm. 'What's up,' he asked. 'She's not sick, is she?'

'Ritzo,' Grandmother said, 'we are neighbours, are we not?'

'Who says otherwise?' Ritzo replied indignantly.

'And I have always thought of you as a *kyrios*, a gentleman, an honest man, wouldn't you say?'

'And I have always behaved that way towards you, Lella.'

23

Grandmother then took the unfortunate hen by the legs and swung it to and fro under the nose of the astonished Ritzo. 'Well,' she said, 'I'll agree that's how it used to be, but unless you do something about this' – she stabbed at the swinging bird with her index finger – 'I'll be sorely tempted to think otherwise.'

To say that Ritzo was struck dumb would be an understatement. When he eventually found his voice he was as mad as she. 'What are you saying, woman, eh, eh? You just explain yourself. Charging me with being dishonest, are you! Me, Ritzo Spastis.'

'Explain yourself . . . explain yourself,' Grandmother mocked. 'It is you who should be doing the explaining. You sold me these chickens, you boasted to have the best layers in all the Peloponnese.' She stared at Ritzo triumphantly. 'Now tell me that you didn't know they were barren. Well, they are. Every one of them.'

First Ritzo's face went white, then crimson. 'How dare you accuse me of such a thing!' he roared, giving as good as he'd got.

But Grandmother was not in the least bit shaken. 'Then why haven't I had more than a handful of eggs from them since you sold them to me? Tell me that, if you can.'

'Why don't you ask the rooster that mounts them?' Ritzo yelled at her.

Grandmother felt then that things had gone far enough. 'Right,' she said, 'let's talk about this like good Christians.'

So Ritzo asked us into his yard and while his wife treated us to spoonfuls of chewy vanilla confectionery dipped in tall glasses of iced water, Grandmother and Ritzo talked chickens.

'But Lella,' Ritzo said, 'how is it that there are no eggs when every morning I hear them cackle? I hear them, I tell you. Mine, yours, everyone's. I've sold chickens to most people in this neighbourhood and the only ones not to lay are yours.'

'The noise they make has no bearing on the amount of eggs they lay.' Grandmother was still sticking to her guns.

Ritzo scratched his head. 'Those birds are good layers,' he insisted.

They stayed silent for a while. We sucked on the mound of vanilla at the end of our spoons and waited to see what would happen next. Suddenly Ritzo jumped up from his chair. 'I got it,' he shouted. Marko choked on his vanilla and almost upset his glass of water. Ritzo's sudden leap must have startled him.

Grandmother looked expectantly at Ritzo. 'Well?'

'Lella, my good neighbour,' Ritzo exclaimed, beaming at her, 'your chickens aren't barren. They do lay eggs but someone or something is picking them off right under your nose.' He threw out his arms. 'It's the only logical explanation.'

'You mean a fox, or something like that?'

'Something like that.'

Grandmother considered it. 'Could be you are right,' she conceded.

'Tell you what. I'll come and check over your hen-house myself,' Ritzo offered.

'Right,' Grandmother agreed. 'Seems fair enough to

me. Well, goodbye, neighbour. Come on, children.'

We trooped home in the same order as we'd come. The only difference was that this time Marko trailed a long way behind the rest of us – which was not like him.

Ritzo did come and check over our hen-house and declared it sound. After that the hens began to lay, and for a time we had enough eggs both to eat and sell, but it didn't last. A couple of months later the situation was the same as before. Half-a-dozen eggs on some days and none at all on others. Grandmother did not go back to Ritzo. She hung a blue bead on the door of the hen-house, convinced that someone had given our chickens the evil eye.

In the village things were becoming serious. One day Old Cyclops the Chief of Police, came to the school and stood listening while the schoolmaster tried to explain about a law that had just been passed. It stated that anyone helping or hiding a partisan, whether KKE or ELLAS,* had no right to a trial and would be shot on sight. The schoolmaster did as he was told – he had to – but we could see that he didn't like it. That put him on the wrong side of Cyclops and it was not a good side to be on.

That made Paul, Marko and me wonder whether we should tell them, at home, about the crates of rifles we'd seen in the cave, but somehow we just couldn't. The way things were made us feel there was more safety in silence. One day Stavro, a man from the village whose

*Two separate Communist parties.

26

wife had just died, came to buy flowers for a wreath. We had a lovely garden, thanks to Aunt Hercules having such green fingers, and Stavro said that someone had told someone else, who'd told him, that an order had come from Athens giving the Chief of Police free powers of arrest.

Aunt Hercules would have none of it. 'Someone farts here and it's heard in Athens,' she retorted.

'But the one who told it got it from someone at the station.'

'Rumours,' our aunt insisted. 'You'd think people would have other things to do than go about spreading rumours. We live in a democracy, don't we?'

'But there is a war on. You can't deny it.'

Aunt Hercules snipped off another white carnation. 'Not a war,' she said. 'Not a war, Stavro, just a skirmish.'

And why not a skirmish? I thought. Perhaps it is the dregs of the big war, being cleaned up. Like punishing those who had worked with the Germans. Some women in the village had had all their hair cut off for going with German and Italian soldiers. That kind of thing. But if this was a new war, then who was the enemy? No foreign soldiers had marched across our borders since the other ones had left. No orders in strange languages rang through the village. The shootings and the beatings had stopped and we were once more allowed to be out after dark. But now there was a law that said people could be shot on sight, like mad dogs, and up in the hills crates of guns were being hidden in caves. So who was going to use them on whom? Sides, always sides. Someone was right and someone else was wrong. And the guns in that cave were to be used to settle the dispute.

I looked around our village and saw the same people that I'd seen all my life: neighbours, relatives, friends, our teacher, the priest, the doctor, the butcher, the baker, the barber, Anna's grocery store. Some I liked, some were awkward to deal with, and some were downright objectionable, but still we managed to exist side by side. Occasionally there were squabbles – the kind that neighbours have – but it's like that in small places where everyone knows everyone else.

I tried to make sense of it all and to find someone I could think of as an enemy. And suddenly I thought of the one person, or three persons to be precise, whom I hadn't known all my life and who were newcomers to the village – our new Chief of Police, his stuck-up wife with her painted lips and dyed hair, and their brat, Aristo. He was my age, tall and handsome in an arrogant kind of way, with a soft mouth, wavy black hair, a straight, strong nose and green eyes – or rather, eye, because like his father he had only one real eye. The other one was made of glass. Paul, Marko and I wondered if glass eyes were something one caught. Like warts and verrucas.

Most village children kept clear of Aristo. He was a bully and did not care who knew it. Like most bullies he had to have someone to hide behind when things got rough and so he had put together a gang of ruffians like himself. They called themselves 'The Warriors' and out of school they carried shields to drive home the point.

Father and son, they were one and the same. Yes, I thought, that's when the change had begun. Shortly after they'd come to the village.

Chapter Six

We had not forgotten the cave. It was always on our minds but autumn had crept up on us, and school and bad weather put a stop to more secret jaunts into the hills. To cap it all, I was in my last year at school. I had promised to try and make it to the *gymnasio** and so I spent a lot of time with my nose in my books. I would be taking the exam in the summer and felt far from ready. Most of my class, especially the girls, had decided that they'd had enough of school but Grandmother thought twelve was too early to give up education. She said it was a disgrace that the Government had not yet put up the school-leaving age to at least fourteen.

One day while we were talking about it, Aunt Hercules said jauntily: 'I don't see why Andi has to go to the *gymnasio*. In a few years she will marry and then it will all have been for nothing.'

Grandmother looked at her as if she wanted to kill her. 'Education is never "for nothing",' she snapped. 'Take Cassie . . .'

'Yes, let's take Cassie' (Cassie, or Cassandra, was my

*Grammar school.

mother). 'You sent her to university and she has left you her brats to bring up while she gallivants in the mountains playing the great revolutionary.'

'You could have gone to university, too, if you hadn't gone and got married at fifteen.'

'I don't remember you trying to stop me,' replied Aunt Hercules bitterly.

Grandmother gave her a furious look. 'How could I, when you eloped with that . . . that peasant to Salonica? Then, when he'd had his fun, I had to come and pick up the pieces.'

Aunt Hercules's lips began to tremble. I looked at Marko. Like Paul and me, he was stunned. I suppose I should have taken him and Paul out the room but I couldn't bear to move.

'I didn't ask you to come,' Marko's mother replied with pride.

Grandmother sniffed the air like a mule getting ready to kick. 'No, you didn't. The village where you lived did, though. Come and take her away, they wrote. If you love your daughter, then come and take her away from here. And I went and found you in with the goats clutching your poor idiot child,' she nodded towards Aki, 'and about to give birth. And while you lived in the goat pen, your husband was playing host to his new woman in your house.'

Aunt Hercules had begun to cry softly. I took Paul and Marko by the hand and led them outside. I thought it would be better if we left Grandmother and Aunt Hercules to rake over things that had nothing to do with us by themselves.

Outside, Marko too began to cry, but I pretended not to notice and suggested we go in search of the gang. The thing was that Aristo and his Warriors had given us plenty of hassle throughout the term and made us thoroughly sick of them. Hardly a day went by without someone being beaten up by those hooligans. Aristo didn't do any of the actual beating himself. Oh no, he only gave the orders and the gang carried them out. In short, they did his dirty work for him.

In the end the beatings became so frequent that Paul, Marko and I decided to form our own gang. Anyone who wanted to could join. Well, we got Mathi, the barber's son; Tom, the baker's boy; Iphigenia (Gina for short) who was twice the size of any of us but was in my class at school; Ritzo's twins George and Laki; Louka, whose father was a boatman; Lou-Lou who was in love with my brother Paul; Tina, who, like us, had always lived with her grandmother; Leoni the carpenter's son and his sister Drina; Dimitri the orphan, who helped to dig graves; Basil, the butcher's errand-boy, and his brother Nico. There were sixteen of us and fourteen of them but some of Aristo's lot were older than us and that evened things out.

We called ourselves 'The Skylarks' and spread it about that we were looking for trouble. And sometimes we got it. Like when we dared the Warriors to meet us in the cemetery at midnight. They went pale but there was no way that they could refuse without showing themselves up as the cowards they were. It was a cold night with dense, fast-moving cloud. One moment the cemetery would be bathed in liquid silver, the next it was plunged into almost total darkness as the mass of cloud passed over the white face of the moon. It was a creepy night all right. Dimitri, who knew the cemetery like the back of his hand, led us to a grave that he'd been digging earlier in the day. There we put our plan for scaring the pants off the Warriors into action. We took an old white sheet that Gina had begged off her mother and pulled it over Dimitri. Then we helped him into the open grave and went to hide behind the bushes and hedges in and around the cemetery.

We didn't have long to wait. As the clock in the clocktower above the village struck twelve the Warriors filed in through the gates, their eyes darting everywhere at once. It was easy to see that they were scared legless. What came next was a treat. Suddenly, just as the moon disappeared behind a particularly heavy cloud, Dimitri shot out of the grave in which he'd been hiding. It was horrible. The whole thing. The crosses and the marble angels silhouetted against the sky, the graves half in and half out of the shadows . . . but the most horrible vision of all was Dimitri the arch-ghoul himself. Very slowly, but with ghastly deliberation, his face lit up by the torch that he was holding under his chin, he moved towards Aristo and his gang . . .

It really was ghostly and too much for the Warriors. One brave act, a tug at the sheet covering Dimitri, would have been enough to stop them going crazy, but they were in no mood to stay and investigate the Ghoul. Whimpering and sobbing with fright they turned on their heels and poured out of the cemetery gates as if an entire army of ghosts had risen and were snapping at their heels. Faster and faster they ran, and I bet they didn't stop until they were safely tucked in their beds with their blankets over their heads.

Chapter Seven

When we were sure that the Warriors would not be returning, we left our hiding-places and congratulated Dimitri for having been an A1 ghoul.

'But weren't you scared down there?' Lou-Lou asked him, at the same time moving nearer Paul. She really was sweet on him.

Dimitri laughed. 'The dead don't scare me,' he said. 'The only things that make me legless are wild dogs and Old Cyclops.'

'Better watch out then,' warned Nico, 'because I bet that even now Aristo is working out a plan to get even with all of us.'

'Let him,' put in Gina. Being so big gave her courage. 'Who cares about him and his mongrels anyway?' She climbed on top of a grave and poured out some of her courage on to us. 'Are we afraid of Cyclops, big or small?' she shouted.

'No!' we shouted back.

'Are we afraid of wild dogs?'

'No!'

'Are we going to let ourselves be pushed around?'

'No!'

'Do we stand together?'

'Yes!'

And that's how it was. We were as free as air and proud to have turned into a force worth reckoning with.

Aristo's revenge came soon after. Of course, having lost face so completely he had to do something to show that he was still in charge, and of course he picked on those younger and smaller and more hungry than himself. That was typical of Aristo, he was all for easy victories. Anyway, one day at school he ordered his thugs to collect the bread from the children in the first two classes, the six- and seven-year-olds. This took even his band of cowards by surprise. True, they were bad, but like us they were poor and knew what it meant to go without one's piece of bread. We all had so little and many had even less than that. Everyone except Aristo knew from experience that this piece of bread was all we had in the way of food. It was what kept us going, our only 'meal', between leaving home in the morning and returning in the evening, when parents would come in from the fields. At worst, that daily piece of bread brought to school would be soaked in water to soften it and sprinkled with salt. At best, it would have been dipped in olive oil and coated with sugar. But what did Aristo know of hunger? His bread was spread with butter and jam, and in his home his mother cooked both lunch and supper. The police, I thought, must be like the army. They look after their own.

The children, terrified of Aristo because his father was a policeman, gave up their bread without protest.

But that wasn't enough for Aristo. Perhaps he thought that he hadn't shown enough 'muscle'. So, taking each piece that was handed to him, he flung it to the ground and dug it into the dust with the heel of his shoe. 'I wouldn't give that to my dog,' he sneered, boring his good eye into the tearful faces of his small victims who had watched the destruction of their bread in silence.

'And you are not fit to lick a dog's ass,' I yelled, and for the first time in my life I knew what it meant to 'see red'. I hurled myself at Aristo and the expression of astonishment in his good eye and the blank wonder of the glass one almost made me laugh.

But he recovered fast. Getting hold of my pigtails, he jerked my head back so hard that I was sure it would come clear off my neck. Keeping a tight grip on my hair, he was slowly forcing me to the ground and would have put the boot in had I not sunk my teeth into his plump leg. With a roar of real pain he let go of my pigtails and clasped his leg instead. My teeth marks could clearly be seen, and a steady trickle of blood travelled down his leg and on to his neat white socks. 'You'll pay for this, you red bitch,' he screamed, making me aware, for the first time, that I had more than one name.

When I got home after school I told Grandmother what had happened and asked her why Aristo had called me a 'red bitch'.

'That boy should have his mouth washed out with soap,' snapped Aunt Hercules. Then she turned to me. 'You should be ashamed of yourself, Antigone,' she said. 'Why couldn't you have let things be? Why must you always fight everyone?'

'But he took their bread,' I protested.

'And who are you to stand up for them? Would anyone have done that for you?'

I looked at Grandmother. 'I was right to fight Aristo, wasn't I?' I asked her.

She nodded. 'Yes, my girl. You did right to fight him. He is bad, that one.'

This irritated Aunt Hercules. 'That's right,' she mocked, 'that's right. You just go ahead and encourage her. She'll get us all into trouble one of these days, see if she won't.'

Grandmother waved to her to be quiet, then she put her arm around me and pulled me down on to her lap. 'Andi,' she said, 'your aunt is right. Aristo and his people are not like us. A policeman never forgets a wrong. So I'm asking you to be very careful from now on and remember that you haven't made just one enemy but three. By beating Aristo you didn't humiliate just him, but his mother and father too. Sooner or later they'll find a way to get even with you . . . and with us.'

This reminded me of that 'red bitch' business. 'What's a "red bitch", Grandmother?'

'That's what some people call a woman who is a communist.'

'What's that?'

'It's what your mother and father got us into, that's what,' exclaimed Aunt Hercules angrily.

'Be quiet, Hara,' Grandmother ordered her. To me she said, her voice suddenly harsh, almost threatening, 'I forbid you to get into any more fights with Aristo. Do I make myself clear?'

I caught her anger. 'I'll fight him if I have to,' I yelled, 'and no one is going to stop me.'

Then Grandmother did something which she had never done before. She grabbed me by the arms and shook me till my teeth rattled. 'You will not, Andi, you will not. For all our sakes.'

'I will,' I shouted back. 'I will. I will.'

And then Grandmother did something else that was new to me. She hit me. I stared at her as if she were a stranger. Then I broke away from her and ran off to cry by myself in the branches of the old eucalyptus tree at the bottom of the garden.

When Grandmother slipped into bed beside me that night, I turned to the wall and pretended to be asleep. She didn't try to talk me round or to apologize for having hit me. She just stroked my hair and kissed me goodnight like she always did, and that made the floodgates inside me open for the second time that day and I sobbed and sobbed while she went on stroking my head in silence, melting the ice inside me just by being there.

Chapter Eight

School ended a week before Christmas. Then that too came and went and suddenly it was already New Year's Eve. We did not believe in St Nicholas and his sack of gifts any more, though we did not let on to the grown-ups because we didn't want to disillusion them. But we did believe in presents from Grandmother and Aunt Hercules. And they never let us down. We were poor and at war once again, but somehow St Nicholas would come by this year, too, just as he had done every New Year's Day throughout the last war.

'I'd like a whole pig on a spit,' announced Marko, his mind being always on food.

'I want an atlas,' I said, 'and a pair of patent pumps with just a bit of a heel.' A long time ago my mother had had a pair of shoes like that and they had become an obsession with me.

'How dull,' Paul said unkindly. 'I want a tank. One that spits fire when you wind it up. It has a turret that swings from side to side as it goes along and it moves on caterpillar tracks.'

Now it was my turn to be unkind. 'There isn't such a thing, stupid,' I replied.

'There is too,' Paul retorted triumphantly. 'Aristo has got one.'

I felt my eyes become two narrow slits in my face.

'How do you know that?'

'Taki told me.'

Taki was one of Aristo's thugs. I was furious that my brother should even have looked his way, let alone talked with him. I decided to let him know how I felt right away. 'You are not to speak to him ever again,' I warned him.

Being one-and-a-half years older than Paul, I felt I had the right to tell him what he could and could not do. That's not how he saw it. 'I'll talk to whoever I like,' he threw at me.

I grabbed his arm and twisted it behind his back. 'You'll do as you are told,' I said grimly. 'Now say you'll not talk to him again.'

'Let go,' yelled my little brother. 'Let go or . . .'

'Or what?' I pushed his arm a fraction higher up his back.

'Oh . . .' he screamed, 'that hurts.'

'It's meant to. Now promise you won't go near any of Aristo's hooligans.'

But he wasn't my brother for nothing. 'No,' he screamed at me, his voice dark with pain, 'no I won't. I hate you . . . I hate you and I wish Mother was here and . . .'

I let go of him then and I was angry and ashamed of myself for the way I'd behaved. I might as well have been Aristo or one of his bullies. 'I am sorry, Paul,' I said.

He stopped sobbing and wiped his eyes on the sleeve of his sweater. 'You didn't have to twist so hard,' he mumbled, his voice still trembling a little.

'No, I didn't,' I admitted, 'I'm sorry if I hurt you.'

'It's all right,' he murmured without looking at me.

I put out my hand and ruffled his soft brown curls and right then I, too, wished that our mother would come back to us and take us in her arms and tell us that she would never leave us again.

Chapter Nine

We drank to the New Year at the stroke of midnight with the sweet wine that Grandmother had brought out of the cupboard like a magician brings rabbits out of an empty hat. (I swear there hadn't been a bottle there when she'd asked me to get out the glasses.) We touched glasses and wished each other a Happy New Year and a speedy end to the war and that our mother and father would come home and that all the children in the world should have mothers and fathers who would never, never go away and leave them. Finally we wished, as we did every New Year, that Aki should be given the use of his arms and legs and be like other boys.

After a while Grandmother said that it was time for bed and I asked if Paul and Marko could sleep in with us just this once, and she said yes, that would be all right provided we didn't talk all night. She said that if we went to bed quietly she might even tell us a story when she came up. And we were good. We felt a strange need to be together this particular night because for some reason we were thoughtful when we should have been carefree, and melancholy when we should have been happy.

And so we undressed and went to bed, the boys on a

43

mattress on the floor, lying head to toe, and I in my usual place beside Grandmother. But before she'd had time to begin a story we started telling her about our gang and about Aristo and his gang, and that reminded me that she'd never answered my question about what a communist was.

'Hm . . .' she replied, 'it's a bit late but I suppose I'd better try to explain it to you or we shan't ever get to sleep tonight.' She paused for a moment to gather her thoughts. 'To be a communist,' she began, 'is to want all good things for all people . . . At least, that's the idea,' she added as a kind of afterthought.

'Then it's not a bad thing to be,' I said, relieved that it didn't mean anything worse than that.

'That depends whether one lives in the real world or not,' retorted Grandmother.

We looked at one another. She'd sailed well beyond us. 'We don't understand,' I said, speaking for Paul and Marko as well.

'I don't expect you do.' She leaned on her elbow. 'Let me put it like this. Aristo and his kind of people have all they could wish for: enough to eat and drink, clothes on their backs, shoes on their feet, the right schools and opportunities for their children. In short, they've always had enough of everything and they like to think that it will always be so. Anyway, being so fortunate, one would think that they might want to share some of the good things they have with others less fortunate than themselves. But far from it. If any of you went up to Aristo and said to him: "Listen here, Aristo, be a good neighbour and give me some of that bread that

44

you are about to give your dog", he'd think you mad. In fact he'd probably set the dog on you for being so cheeky.'

'I'd share my bread if I was asked to,' Paul said gravely.

'And why would you do that?' Grandmother challenged him.

'Because I couldn't eat if I knew someone else was hungry,' Paul replied indignantly.

I nodded but Marko was strangely quiet and his face had gone all red as if he'd suddenly developed a fever.

'So,' Grandmother went on, 'sharing, or owning things together, is what it's all about. To be a communist means to share and share alike.'

'Then it is a good thing,' I insisted.

'The concept, the idea, is a good one but it is something that one must arrive at of one's own free will,' she replied, her voice taut with sudden anger. 'To run before one can walk only leads to trouble.'

The boys looked blank but I thought I was beginning to understand. 'Is that what this new war is about?' I asked.

Grandmother sighed. 'That's one aspect,' she said.

'What's the other?'

But like the boys, Grandmother had had enough of politics. 'Look,' she said, 'it's much too complicated to go into now. I am not even sure that I understand it myself. What I do understand, though, is that we need time . . . not more war. Communism is an ideal – not a workable reality. Not yet, anyway.'

And now she had lost me, too, but I had just one

45

more question for her. 'Is our mother a communist too? And you, Grandmother, and our father and Aunt Hercules . . .

'. . . and Jesus?' Marko slipped in.

I shot him a hard look. 'And Aunt Dina?' I continued. Somehow I didn't feel like including Uncle Tasso.

Grandmother boxed her pillow into shape before she put her head down on it. 'Hm,' she said, 'hm . . .' I suppose she thought she'd keep it simple this time.

Chapter Ten

The next day, New Year's Day, we woke up to the smell of oranges and honey, cloves and cinnamon. We dressed quickly, gave ourselves a catlick, and went down to the kitchen to see what was cooking. There we found Aunt Hercules not cooking but baking. She was mixing the ingredients for *melomakarouna*, the rich brown seasonal cakes, into a large bowl with stiff angry movements as if it was something she was doing because she had to and not because she wanted to. She poured in the oil, the ouzo and the pressed orange juice carelessly, spilling a good deal of it on to the floor. Then she stirred it all together with resentment and ugly grimaces. Last came the cinnamon, the cloves and the ground walnuts which she mixed in with the other things with a final show of fury.

Nearby a pita, the round New Year's bread, had been put aside to rise. Outside in the yard Grandmother was getting ready to light the oven.

'Why are you baking again, Aunt?' I asked. 'Have the rats got the last lot, or something?'

'Or something. . .' muttered our aunt without looking up.

I looked at Paul and Marko. My brother was as puzzled as I was. Marko shot to the door. He said that he was going to help Grandmother light the oven. Grandmother seldom bothered to light that oven because it needed so much wood to get it going, but today the one in the village was shut so she had no choice but to bake at home. But why were we baking again today when we'd done it all several days ago?

Children from all over the village had marched to the bakery in long lines with their trays balanced on their heads, their eyes glowing with excitement, not least because of the coin hidden in the pita. 'My mother put a whole drachma* into our pita,' someone had piped. 'Ours was a brand-new one,' someone else shouted. 'My uncle who was in America gave us a five-drachma for ours,' said another. 'That's nothing. My mother put a gold sovereign in ours . . .' That could only have come from Aristo. As usual he had to have the last word.

Aunt Hercules had mixed a drachma coin into ours, one that I had polished until it shone like a mirror. I wondered if the rats had got it, too. I wanted to ask Aunt Hercules about it but her stern, closed face put me off. Why was she sulking, anyway? We couldn't help it if the rats had got to things.

I gestured to Paul to follow and we went outside. Grandmother had got the oven going and Marko was wiping sweat and soot from his face. 'He certainly is a good blower,' Grandmother said and patted Marko on the head. 'Lungs like a pair of bellows. Wouldn't have

*A unit of Greek currency.

got it going without him.' Marko beamed. His face was red from the effort of blowing and he looked like a cherub on an ikon. Marko was much more healthy-looking than Paul and me. We were always pale except in the summer when our paleness was hidden behind a tan. Marko, on the other hand, looked like a prize apple all the year round.

We weren't going to be needed for a while so we set off for the square hoping to meet others from our gang. When we arrived we found that most of them were already there and in splendid spirits. A while later Aristo and his gang sauntered in, too. He was also in good form because he and his louts came up to us and began to shake our hands, wishing us a Happy New Year. Some of our lot didn't want to but I told them that it was a truce we were shaking on, not a peace treaty, and that brought them round. But it was easy to see that they didn't like it.

We spent the morning playing hide-and-seek and catch with them, and everyone was on their best behaviour. I thought how easy it was to get on with people, if everyone minded their own business. Then our mother and father would be with us instead of up in the hills, and Aristo would be our friend and his father would chase real criminals instead of people who had done nothing wrong except think differently from him.

We had intended to be good all day, when, just before noon, little Aleko, Notta the Herb-picker's seven-year-old grandson, came to the fountain to fill his granny's pitcher. As if at a given signal we moved around the little boy and began to stare at the pitcher under the tap. Aleko, afraid that we were about to use his pitcher as a target for our slings, moved closer to it and looked at us with dark, worried eyes.

'Hi, Aleko, Happy New Year to you,' said Tom the baker's boy.

'Happy New Year,' Aleko answered shyly.

'Look here, Aleko,' Tom continued, 'how would you like to make two pitchers from one?'

Aleko's eyes became as large as dinner plates in his face, but he shook his head. 'Think how pleased your grandmother would be,' cooed Tom.

'St Nicholas will leave an extra present for you if you do,' put in Gina.

'A tank that fires real, live shells,' Aristo joined in, his handsome face one great malicious grin.

That did it. Little Aleko nodded and Tom at once set about demonstrating the technique. Taking hold of his earlobes he pulled three times, then asked Aleko to do the same. Aleko obeyed. 'Now,' Tom said, 'you have to pick up your pitcher, spit on it three times, then let go of it. Then you must tug at your ears again before it hits the ground or it won't work. Ready?'

Aleko nodded, trembling with excitement. Tom gave him a friendly pat on the back. 'That's all there's to it. Except, don't forget to shut your eyes and count to ten.'

Aleko followed Tom's instructions to the letter. He pulled at his poor ears until they were red, let go of the pitcher, shut his eyes and waited for it to duplicate itself as Tom had said. When, at last, he opened them again he was alone, his pitcher and his day in pieces.

I am ashamed to say that we laughed until tears ran

down our cheeks and our stomachs began to ache with the effort of it. 'Bet he'll keep a better hold on his pitcher from now on,' said Tom heartlessly, as though the lesson poor Aleko had learned that day might prove useful to him later in life.

Chapter Eleven

Late in the afternoon we were given our presents. I got
the atlas but not the shoes. They'd only been a dream
anyway. Paul got a new pencil-case with five coloured
pencils in it. He loved to draw and didn't really mind
not having a tank like Aristo's – like my shoes, the tank
too had been a dream. Marko got a mouth organ, something he'd wanted for a long time, though of course
he'd rather have had the pig.

In the evening we sat down to our New Year's dinner in
the *sala*. Normally this room was out of bounds to us
children. We were only allowed in on special occasions,
like today, or when there happened to be guests visit-
ing. It was a lovely, exciting room because it was for-
bidden to us. The rest of the house was almost bare, but
in the *sala* there were rugs on the floor and tapestries
embroidered by Aunt Hercules on the walls, small
marble-topped tables with photographs on them (one
was a wedding photograph of our mother and father), a
huge mirror set in a splendid gilded frame, a wardrobe
so big it reminded us of the cave whenever we looked at
it, a low wooden chest which had once held Grand-

mother's dowry, and a commode with six drawers.

In the middle of the room was the great mahogany table with its six matching chairs: a present that Grandfather had brought for Grandmother from one of his journeys. The top of it was so polished that one could see one's face in it but today it was covered over by a dazzlingly white linen cloth with matching napkins which Grandfather had brought back from Ireland. We were careful not to soil it as we tucked into the roast chicken, the crispy golden potatoes, the salads topped with cheese from the *stani* and the thick, moist slices of Pita smelling of butter and eggs. It goes without saying that the coin went to Marko. I don't know why, but if there was anything to be found or won, one could bet one's life it would go to Marko.

'What are you going to do with it, Marko?' we asked him.

Marko thought for a moment, then he said, 'I think I'll invest it in a packet of chewing gum.'

'Chewing gum,' we shouted with one voice.

Marko smiled shyly. 'That's right,' he replied, 'and then for five lepta* I'll let anyone who wants to have a chew of it.'

'That son of yours will either become a great businessman or a great crook,' Grandmother said. Then she added, quite wickedly I thought, 'It comes to the same thing, if you ask me.'

But Aunt Hercules wasn't at all put out. 'My boy knows how to look after himself,' she said, puffed up with pride.

*100 lepta = 1 drachma.

'As long as he doesn't step over too many corpses to do it,' replied Grandmother drily.

We were slouching in our chairs after the meal. Our stomachs weren't used to so much food all at once and we felt a little ill. Also we'd become dizzy from the wine, though Grandmother had diluted ours with water. I suppose we would have fallen asleep had Grandmother not suddenly put her finger to her lips and gestured to Aunt Hercules to switch off the light. All at once we were wide-awake and on the alert. We had heard of people being arrested in their homes at dead of night and felt sure that the Chief of Police was on his way up to us. I moved close to Paul and put my arms around him. He leaned against me, his hand digging into mine, and I thought how small he was, still, and how little difference it made that he was a boy and I a girl. Marko went to stand next to his mother and she put her hand over Aki's mouth to stop him from making any noise.

Minutes later we heard someone on the balcony and the sound of the door-handle being pushed down. Then all was still again, as if whoever had been out there had suddenly disappeared into thin air.

Chapter Twelve

We didn't know he was there until he was in the room with us. Once in the house, even with its creaking boards, he'd been as silent as a cat. In the almost total darkness of the room he was no more than a shadow but we knew him at once.

'Father,' we mouthed silently, too surprised even to cry out, 'Father', and slid out of our chairs and into his arms.

Grandmother lit some candles which she put on the floor so that the light would not be visible from outside. 'Talk,' she said, 'but keep it low.'

'Father,' we kept saying over and over again, still not really convinced that he was here, with us. 'Father, you came.'

'I had to come and wish my brave fighters a Happy New Year. You see, I know what goes on down here.' He was being cheerful for us but in the dim light from the candles we looked into his eyes and saw that the smile stopped short of them. He was tense. Very tense. We could feel that it was an effort for him to smile at all. But he was determined not to spoil the evening for us. 'And would I come on New Year's Day empty-handed?'

He looked at Marko. 'You too, Marko,' he said kindly.

Paul got his tank. Father said it was the most popular toy on sale that year. Like Aristo's, it spat fire, the turret swung round and it moved on caterpillar tracks.

'Thank you, Father, thank you,' whispered Paul, throwing his arms around Father's neck. 'Aristo will choke when he hears that he's not the only one to have a "Chieftain".'

'Who is this Aristo, Paul?' Father asked gently.

'Oh, he's the Chief of Police's son,' replied Paul readily. 'He's a bully and has a gang called the Warriors.' Then he giggled and pointed at me. 'But Andi fought him when he took the bread from the little ones and bit him. You should have seen her, Father, she went for him like a mad dog.'

Now Father was beginning to laugh. 'Did she bite him?' he asked.

Paul nodded, his curls dancing. 'She did, Father. She got him in the leg and you could see the teeth marks for a whole week afterwards.' He was exaggerating, of course.

Father put his arm around my waist and drew me closer to him. 'I heard you fought with him,' he said, 'but no one told me you bit him.'

I nodded. 'I wouldn't have done it if he hadn't pulled my plaits,' I defended myself.

'It's all right, my dove. I wasn't getting at you. Only if I had known that you've become so brave and serious I would have brought you something different.' He pulled a parcel wrapped in coloured paper out of his rucksack and handed it to me. 'As it is, I'm afraid you'll have to make do with this.'

I opened it. It was a doll, dressed in pink organza with arms and legs that moved and eyes that opened and closed. It was a wonderful doll and only last year it would have been the perfect present. But I was eleven years old and in my last year at school, my mind on the coming exams and on the war, and suddenly I felt very old. It seemed that the time for playing with dolls had passed me by.

'I am sorry,' my father said, apologizing for the doll. 'I had no idea you'd grown so.' He sounded so sad, as if he had lost something precious, that it almost broke my heart to hear him.

I put my wet cheek against his stubbly one and threw my arms around him. What did I care about presents? All that mattered was that we were together, our arms around one another, his kisses on our faces, the love he had for us in his heart. 'Stay, Father, stay, stay, stay,' I wanted to shout, but it was his day too, and I didn't want to spoil it for him.

Marko got half-a-dozen tin soldiers. He thanked my father shyly, then he and Paul went off into another part of the room to play war. Suddenly I was sorry for Marko and glad that my father had remembered him. It must be awful not to have a father even if like ours, his visits were as rare as swallows in winter.

Chapter Thirteen

'Father, will you be going away again?' asked Paul between battles.

'I'm afraid so, my boy.'

'Your father took a terrible risk coming here tonight,' Grandmother put in.

Father looked up. 'What's worse, I've put the lives of all of you at risk, too.'

'How's that, Father?'

He took my hand. I don't know which of us he was trying to comfort. 'A partisan,' he said, 'may be shot on sight, like a stray dog,' he looked at us gravely, 'and so may anyone harbouring a partisan. Now do you understand the danger that we are all in?'

I nodded and remembered that months ago Old Cyclops had made the schoolmaster read the new order from some newspaper or other. I told Father. He nodded. 'I see that I don't have to say any more,' he said. 'but keep your eyes open, children, and never volunteer to say more than is necessary to anyone. You don't have to be rude to people but if you find the way they ask you things uncomfortable, play dumb.'

'Like we do when we are at Uncle Tasso's?' Paul volunteered.

Father looked at Grandmother. 'Yes, just like when you are at Uncle Tasso's,' he repeated.

'Who else should we look out for, Uncle?' said Marko.

My father raised and lowered his shoulders in a gesture that suggested the list was endless. Then he looked into our eyes as if he wanted us to pay special attention to what he was about to say. 'I don't want to frighten you,' he replied, 'but the fact is that you have to suspect all and no one. Neighbours, friends . . . people you've known all your life. That's the kind of war this is. One careless word, one look out of place, could mean someone's life. Remember that.'

'Then we mustn't show anyone the presents you brought us,' Paul said. I looked at him and swelled with pride at the way he'd caught on. Father too was pleased. 'That's it, son,' he said. 'Glad to see there are no flies on you.' He turned to Marko. 'Or you,' he added, not wanting our cousin to feel left out.

'Were you and Aunt Cassie together in the mountains?' Marko asked.

Father looked at Paul and me. 'I haven't said anything about your mother,' he said, 'because I'm not allowed to and because the less you know the better.' Then he grinned, a wide, full grin packed with mischief. 'But I hear that she sends you her love, all of you.' That made us all laugh and laugh and the tension was broken and we felt happy and full of hope, like one should at the beginning of a new year. Then Father told us that he had come to see us now because he would be going away and could not say when he might be back.

59

'Are you going back up to the mountains?' Paul asked.

Father shook his head. 'No,' he answered, 'my work lies elsewhere now.'

'Then where are you going?', Paul insisted.

Father hesitated. Then he said, 'I am going to Egypt.'

Grandmother choked, as if she'd got a bone stuck in her throat. 'And how do you think you'll get there?' she wheezed.

'By boat,' Father replied casually, trying hard to sound as if he was going on a picnic to the monastery across the bay.

'And how do you plan to get a boat with everyone looking for you?'

'It's all been taken care of.'

'What have you taken care of?'

'The boat. I've got it.'

'You've got the boat.' Grandmother was acting real dense but perhaps she was recovering from the shock of Father going to Egypt. But he was patient with her. 'Yes, Lella,' he said slowly, as if talking to a child, 'I've got the boat. It's hidden under the jetty.'

Grandmother drew herself up in her chair, fully recovered now. 'What kind of boat is it?' she inquired almost haughtily.

'Used to be a pilot,' Father informed us. 'She is two metres long and not quite a metre wide. She can carry up to one hundred kilos of cargo, has a mast, a mainsail and a jib, and can reach up to five miles an hour when the winds are with her.'

'And what happens when there's no wind?'

'Then I'll have to row.'

'You mean to row to Egypt in a dinghy?' Grandmother suddenly shouted. 'Tell me, how far do you think you'll get?'

'I'll make for Turkey first, then I'll hug the coast to Alexandria.'

'It's madness, Antony. Sheer madness,' exclaimed Aunt Hercules, and spread her cardigan over Aki who'd fallen asleep in his chair.

Father looked almost apologetic when he answered. 'I've no choice, Hara. I'm too well-known here now to be of any real use.'

'And what will you do in Egypt, Father?' I asked him.

He stroked my face with the back of his hand. 'I'll join others who think the way I do and together we'll work towards putting an end to this war.'

'Seems to me you are doing your best to get yourself drowned!' Grandmother cut in bitterly. Then she pushed her nose into a corner of her apron and made the sound of an elephant with a cold.

Father rose and went to her and put his arms around her. 'Come now, Lella,' he said, 'we've been through worse, you and I, haven't we?'

'It's your children I am thinking of, my son. Poor mites, they might as well be orphans.'

Father returned to sit by us. 'Well, they are not,' he said firmly, 'and once this war is over, Cassie and I will make it up to them.' He drew us to him. 'Yes, when this is over, we'll never, never be apart again. Nothing, no one, will dare to separate us then.'

'And how long will it take you to reach Alexandria?' Aunt Hercules asked.

Father shrugged his shoulders. 'I don't know, Hara. Weeks, perhaps even months. At sea so much depends on luck.'

'What's the name of your boat, Father?' I asked. It seemed important to me that she should have a name. It would be easier to think of her then. It sort of proved that she existed.

'Let me think . . .' Father replied slowly. 'She is very small . . . at sea she won't seem much bigger than a nutshell . . .'

'*The Little Nutshell*,' I cried. 'Oh, Father, let's call her *The Little Nutshell*.'

'Yes . . .' Father agreed. 'Yes. *The Little Nutshell* it is. God bless her . . .'

'. . . and all who sail in her,' we all shouted.

Except Aki, that is. He was in a world of his own.

Chapter Fourteen

A silent farewell, a few hurried kisses and he was gone, swallowed up by the night. Crouching behind a clump of bamboos we waited for *The Little Nutshell* to come out from her hiding-place. A while later, there she was, an impossibly small craft, dangerously low in the water, her mast tapering off into the darkness, the sail furled around the boom and the minute figure of our father at the oars being taken further and further away from us with every stroke. The oars had been wrapped in sacks to keep them from making a noise as they touched the water, and it was so dark, and each stroke so silent, that we wouldn't have seen him if we hadn't known he was there.

And soon we lost sight of him altogether, and it was a miserable trio that ambled back to the house. Even Marko seemed really sad, even though it wasn't his father.

I tried not to cry when I got in, but Grandmother must have sensed how I felt. She didn't say anything, just drew me to her and held me close and suddenly I was all tears and it felt as if I would never laugh again.

Paul, too, cried himself to sleep in the little room next

to ours. I wanted to go to him but Grandmother said that pain, like love, was a very private thing and some people had their own way of dealing with it.

'I can't bear to see Paul hurt,' I sobbed.

Grandmother turned out the light. 'I know,' she said, 'but he's young, he'll heal.'

Chapter Fifteen

School got under way again at the end of January with more homework than ever before, especially for those of us who would be taking examinations. We worked very hard, except Aristo, that is. He never did any homework, he didn't have to, his place in the *gymnasio* was assured. Anyway, as Lou-Lou's father said, 'It's not what you have up here that will get you a place, but who you know and how deep you are prepared to dig into your pocket.'

It rained all through January and February. Then at the beginning of March there was a break in the weather and one Sunday Grandmother suddenly asked us whether we would mind going up to the *stani*. We immediately agreed – trying hard not to sound too eager. Now at last we could go back to the cave.

'I wonder if the guns are still there,' said Paul, thinking aloud. Marko, too, had something on his mind. 'I wonder if there'll be anything special to send this time, too,' he said . . . much too tentatively for him.

'We don't know that there was anything special sent up last time,' I said. 'We couldn't untie the knot to look, remember?'

'Doesn't matter. I still think we took something special last time we went up there,' he replied, sounding sure this time, the way one does when one has found something out.

With a howl and a shriek I threw him to the ground and pinned him down like an insect. 'Don't try that one with me, you little worm,' I hissed at him. 'I'll count to five and you'd better have spilt all you know by the time I've finished or I'll knock you senseless.'

Marko glared at me but he had the good sense to know when he was beaten. 'All right . . . all right . . .' he conceded. 'Get off me and I'll tell you.'

I let him get up and Paul helped to dust him down. 'Right,' I said. 'Get on with it and don't hold anything back.'

'OK,' Marko said, 'here it comes. A few weeks ago I saw Grandmother go upstairs carrying a box of sugar lumps. Well, I waited till she'd come down again then I sneaked upstairs to look for the sugar. I looked everywhere but . . . nothing. I was about to give up when it hit me that I had not searched the *sala*. I didn't think of looking in there because I assumed that it would be locked, as it always is. But when I tried the handle, the door opened as easily as if I'd said "Sesame". I thought I'd start with the wardrobe, and there it was. A box full of sugar lumps. I put some in my pockets . . .'

'. . . and a few in your mouth,' Paul interrupted sarcastically.

'Right,' Marko admitted, 'and then, that over, I thought I'd just peek into another, smaller box that was next to the sugar lumps. I only lifted the lid a little. I was nervous in case Grandmother or any of you should come up but when I saw what was inside I thought I was seeing things. I couldn't believe my eyes. Right in front of me was this treasure. Guess if I was excited!'

He thrust his hand into his pocket and when he brought it out again there it was. A small round coin that could only have been made of gold. The English gold sovereign. I recognized it straightaway. When we'd read about England at school, the schoolmaster had brought one along to show us. I don't know where he'd got it but before the big war lots of people had turned their savings into gold. But I'd never heard that we had any, and especially not a boxful of them.

'Marko,' I said, 'did you have time to count them?'

'No, I was too scared to stay on after I'd found them, so I just put the lid on them and left.'

'How many do you think were in there?'

'I don't know, Andi. But enough to cover the bottom of the box, anyway.'

'How big was the box?'

'It was an old Turkish Delight box.'

'What size?'

'The smallest one.'

That would make it about ten inches long and half as wide again, I thought. Big enough to hold a small fortune. I pointed to the gleaming coin in his hand.

'And what were your plans for that one?' I asked sternly.

'No . . . none . . .' he stammered. 'I . . . I just wanted to hold it for a while.' I believed him. It was just the kind of thing Marko would do. He wasn't a thief and anyway he was pretty well off nowadays. His 'five-lepta chews' had taken off nicely and he was doing far better than any of us had expected. There were days when the queue of children waiting for a 'chew' stretched as far as Ritzo's. Grandmother didn't like it but Aunt Hercules argued that there was nothing wrong in what Marko was doing. They hadn't argued about it and Marko's leather pouch continued to swell.

'Right, Marko,' I said, 'you'd better go and put that coin back. Grandmother is sure to know how many coins there are in that box and it would be bad if she discovered one missing. She obviously doesn't want us to know about the coins or she would have told us.' Like me, the boys were bound to wonder how it was that we were always so short of everything when there was money in the house. Unless . . . unless the money wasn't really ours . . . Perhaps Paul had been thinking along the same lines as me because he suddenly shouted:

'I've got it.'

'Must you yell like that?'

'Listen,' he said, going from yelling to whispering. 'I think Stammo is a kind of middleman.'

'Middleman? For what?'

'Between us and the partisans and . . . we . . . well, Grandmother uses us as couriers when she and Stammo want to exchange messages . . . or when there's been a request for more money from the unit of partisans fighting in this area.'

'So you think it belongs to them and Grandmother is minding it for them?'

'But one needs more money to fight a war than a handful of gold coins,' interrupted Marko, the pragmatist.

'Yes,' I agreed, 'but suppose it's money in reserve for medicines and things like that.'

'And Mother is a nurse,' Paul reminded us.

'And Father did say that they are short of almost everything up there, didn't he?'

Paul nodded and for a while afterwards we sat silent, each with his own thoughts. Then Marko said: 'Jesus.'

We stared at him. 'What's got into you, then?'

'We would all be shot . . .' he said softly. 'If it ever came out, we'd all be shot . . . just like your father said. I mean we are all in it up to our necks and she' (he meant Grandmother) 'is about to send us up there again.'

'In for a penny, in for a pound.' Paul shrugged his shoulders. 'If it makes you feel better, it's less likely that anyone would suspect us than if Grandmother was to take whatever she puts into that bundle up herself. Kids are always taking to the hills to play and to get away from doing chores. Anyway, I'm not scared.'

'Neither am I,' cut in Marko. 'If they come to get us, I know exactly where I'm going to hide.'

'Bet you've already put in plenty of supplies too,' I said sarcastically.

'Of course . . . *I'm* not going to starve to death while I'm hiding, am I?'

Typical Marko, I thought.

Chapter Sixteen

Stammo seemed glad to see us. Once or twice I caught him looking at us. I tried to hold his eyes but every time he'd look away and in the end I was sure I'd imagined it. We didn't stay long. As soon as we'd given him his things (there was no message this time) we said good-bye and made to leave. He asked us to wait a little longer, while he wrapped a piece of feta for Grand-mother. After that we hurried away, anxious to get to the cave. Lately it had become dangerous to roam the hills and we'd been given strict instructions to be back home while it was still light.

And so we began the descent, the eyes of the old shepherd burning holes in our backs. Without really knowing why, I turned round and waved to him. He was funny to look at in his pleated *foustanella*,* leaning on his crook, the heavy woollen cloak held together at the front by a huge safety-pin, a wide oatmeal-coloured sash of wool around his middle, his legs poured into leggings knitted from the same rough wool. On his feet

*Short, pleated white skirt of the kind worn by the Greek National Guard.

he wore sturdy black boots on which he'd fastened some coloured tassels. Suddenly I felt very fond of this brave old man and prayed that if anything happened, his dog, Zak, would be there to protect him.

The hedge hiding the mouth of the cave seemed to have grown more dense since our last visit but in the end, looking as if we'd been mauled by wild animals, we managed to get through it. I had forgotten the torch this time, but luckily Paul had some matches in his pocket. We didn't have a box to strike them on, but any flattish rock in the cave would do. Marko was the first one through.

'Are the guns still there?' shouted Paul, more to hear his own voice than because he expected Marko to reply. Then he too was through, and it was my turn. I was still getting to my feet when a hand was clamped over my mouth, cutting off the air to my lungs and making me thrash about like a fish out of water. Then someone lit a candle and I don't know which was worse, the darkness or the huge wavering shadows on the walls of the cave.

I peered around for Paul and Marko. I eventually made them out at the far end of the cave, pushed up against the wall by a man whose face was wrapped in bandages. Only the eyes, the dark hole of the mouth and the tip of the nose were visible. On the opposite side, near the mouth of the cave, there was a second man, pointing a gun at us. He was leaning against a pile of sacks and moaning as if something was hurting him, though the hand that held the gun seemed steady enough. The third man, the one doing his best to suffocate me, had his left arm in a bloody sling and part of his right earlobe was missing.

'Well, well,' wheezed the one with the gun, 'that's all we need. A pack of curious brats to spread the word.' He pointed at me. 'You can let go of her now.'

The man whose hand was blocking my nose and mouth took it away. I've never tasted anything so delicious as the air that poured into my poor starved lungs. Even if it was dark and stuffy and smelly.

'So, what now? What are we to do with them? If we let them go we're dead men.' The one with the gun grinned. It was a mean smile. 'We can always slit their throats,' he suggested, as casually as if we'd been rabbits or chickens.

'What do you think?' he asked the one still holding me.

The man shrugged his shoulders as if it was all the same to him, but added: 'I've never killed a child before. Not in cold blood anyway.'

'Don't see that we have much choice,' replied the one by Paul and Marko. 'If we let them go they are bound to talk, and then it's thumbs-down for us . . . as well as for a lot of others.'

The one holding me hesitated. 'I don't know,' he said slowly, 'I got two myself . . .'

'This isn't the time to get sentimental,' growled the one with the gun. 'We're not playing Happy Families. There's a war on, remember.'

I don't dare to think what might have happened next, had my brilliant little brother not suddenly thought to say: 'Are you *andartes*?'*

*Partisans.

The gun swung round until it was pointing straight at his head. 'And what's it to you?'

And that's when my little brother put the heads of all three of us on the block. Keeping his eyes on the gun he said: 'Our mother is one.' He'd taken an awful gamble. If he was wrong . . . I didn't dare to breathe lest the sound of my breath should cause the axe to fall. But you bet I prayed. 'Dear God,' I whispered to myself, 'let them be *andartes* and not Monarchists and I'll light a candle to you every Sunday for the rest of my life.'

The gun was lowered a fraction. 'And what is your mother's name?'

Paul cleared his throat. 'Her name is Cassandra Laskari,' he replied calmly.

'And what is she doing with the *andartes*?'

'She is a nurse.'

The man with the gun nodded. 'And you are her children . . . all three of you?'

'Yes.'

The gun rose again. 'I was sure Cassie only had two children,' he said, and there was no mistaking the rising suspicion in his voice.

I thought fast. 'We always think of Marko as a brother,' I slipped in, my face so taut I couldn't even squeeze forth a smile. But the man on the floor could. For the first time there was the hint of a smile on that dark, brooding face.

'Loyalty is a beautiful thing – the best there is,' said the man with the gun. Then he turned to Marko. 'I hope you are worthy of it,' he told him gravely.

After that, things got more relaxed. 'How come you

know of this place?' they wanted to know. We told them we had found it by accident and that we hadn't told anyone, not even those at home or our best friends. No one knew of it.

'Good, then we are still safe here.'

'Don't worry,' Paul told him, 'we won't tell anyone.'

'So, you have been going to the *stani* . . . to old Stammo?'

We nodded. 'And I wouldn't be wrong if I said that you'd worked out what it's all about.' Again we nodded. 'And you understand what it means . . . what it could mean, if . . .?'

'It's all right,' Marko said. 'We are not afraid.'

The wounded man put the gun on the ground beside him. 'You are brave children,' he said. It sounded as if he meant it. Then he changed the subject. 'You must miss your mother,' he said, looking at Paul and me. I felt a rush of hot tears flood my eyes. 'Oh yes,' I whispered. 'Oh yes.'

'Would you like to see her?'

'Please,' Paul replied, his voice hardly audible, then added: 'If it is not too dangerous.'

'It's always dangerous,' the man said seriously, 'but I'll see what can be done. Sunday would be a good day, don't you think?'

'Thank you,' we whispered, 'thank you, thank you, thank you.'

The wounded man suddenly looked worried. 'I said I'd try but I am not promising anything,' he said, as if afraid that he'd already promised too much.

'Please tell her we love her,' Paul said in a small voice.

The man nodded. 'You can be sure I will,' he replied kindly. He motioned towards the mouth of the cave. 'Now go. And make sure you are not seen going through the hedge.'

We'd begun to move towards the opening when he asked: 'Old Stammo give you any cheese, then?' I nodded, puzzled that he should have known about the feta. 'Mind leaving us a bit of it?' I shook my head and handed him the bundle with the piece of cheese Stammo had given us to take to Grandmother. He took it and told us to go through and wait outside. 'Andreas here will bring it to you,' he said.

We crawled out and soon afterwards Andreas, the man with the bandaged face, pushed the red cloth with the remaining cheese through to us. 'Good luck, and keep your eyes open at all times,' he called out, his voice muffled by the bandages and the wall of stone between us.

'You too,' we called back, and moments later we were flying down steep goat-tracks, deep gorges, shallow riverbeds. On and on we ran through heather and myrtle, gorse and pine, until at last we were once again amongst the friendly olives and the lemon and orange trees in Notta the Herb-picker's little orchard and finally through our own gate. There we came to a halt to get our breath back and to swear to a secret.

'Not a word about next Sunday,' I said sternly. 'OK?'
'OK.'

Chapter Seventeen

On Saturday evening Paul and I told Grandmother that we wanted to take a bath and wash our hair. She didn't act at all surprised, just gave us a kind of long look, then she filled the great brass cauldron with water from the well and lit the fire under it. When it was hot she poured some into the tin bath and asked whether we were going in separately or together. I let Paul have his first. He was smaller than me and had less hair to wash and, anyway, lately I'd begun to feel that I didn't want anyone but Grandmother to see me naked.

'I suppose you want your hair in curlers, too?' asked Grandmother when she was drying me.

'Yes, please,' I answered, hoping I hadn't given anything away.

'Such fuss just to go to church. Are you sure you haven't found yourself a young man, my angel?' she teased me.

Grown-ups! Why a young man? Why shouldn't I want to look nice just for myself? 'Don't be so silly, Grandmother,' I snapped at her. 'I want to look different for once, that's all. I'm tired of plaits, they . . . they make me look like a child.'

'Well, well,' shouted Aunt Hercules from her room, 'she'll be demanding a dowry next.'

I wondered how someone as old as Aunt Hercules could be so silly and opted for ignoring anything she said. Grandmother left me to dress and went to get the curlers. She separated my long hair into thin strands, wrapped each one around a curler and rolled it up close to the scalp. When she'd finished she'd done them up so tight that my whole head throbbed.

'Grandmother,' I said crossly, 'you've done them up too tight. I'm going to get a headache, I know I am.'

'Everything has its price,' she replied drily, 'and vanity comes dear.'

I lay on my back all night so as not to disturb the curlers and as a result I slept badly and woke up grouchy. I suppose I was suffering from nerves but I didn't know it then. I was keyed-up for the meeting with Mother and even the most innocent remark seemed to have been designed to annoy me.

'Why,' Grandmother exclaimed as she removed the curlers from my hair and began to brush it, 'you look quite a lady with your hair curled.' But right then I felt very young and very jumpy and a compliment was as good as a curse. So I responded with a grimace, a very unflattering one, and Grandmother finished combing my hair in silence. She didn't speak again until we were about to leave. 'So it's church, is it?' I gave a short nod. 'I haven't been for a while. Perhaps I should come too.'

I looked at Paul who'd just come into the room. 'We've already arranged to meet up with some of the others,' I tried to keep my voice calm and matter-of-fact.

Grandmother folded her arms across her chest and raised her eyebrows into two perfect arches above her eyes. 'I say, you two, isn't Marko going with you?'

I swallowed. I was as taut as a rubber band. Talk of changing tacks. Well, she almost had us off the rails that time.

'Isn't he ready?' Paul asked innocently.

'I don't think he's coming,' I said. 'He hasn't been so keen on going to church lately.'

'Perhaps you are right,' Grandmother answered, her eyes riveted on our faces. It seemed to satisfy her but she insisted on seeing us to the gate and that created yet another problem. The way to the cave lay to the right, the one to the church, left. Of course we turned left but we'd only gone a few steps when Grandmother's voice made us freeze in our tracks.

'Shouldn't you be going right?' she called out, softly, softly, like a cat who's played too long with the mouse and grown tired of the game.

Chapter Eighteen

The cave, when we finally reached it, was empty. There wasn't a trace of anyone or anything having been there. We felt a little silly sitting in a dark dank cave dressed in our Sunday best.

'Are you sure he said Sunday?' Paul asked anxiously.

'Quite certain,' I replied.

'Well,' Paul mumbled, 'he said he'd try. He didn't promise that she would come.'

'It was a kind of promise,' I insisted stubbornly.

'Hm,' said Paul, steeling himself against disappointment.

We stayed silent after that but every once in a while one of us would go to the mouth of the cave and look out. The day, which had begun hazy, turned crystal clear. The hours passed. Ten, eleven, twelve . . . and still no one came. Later, when the light changed from brilliant white to rose pink, we decided not to wait any more. Our mother wasn't coming and we had to get home before the sun set and darkness fell.

We started down in silence, dragging our feet. The disappointment, the bitterness we felt at having been let down, the need to find a place where we might be left to lick our wounds in peace led us, without us being aware of it, up instead of down, so that suddenly we found ourselves on the path to the sheepfold. I suppose that in some way we believed that the old shepherd might be holding the answer or at least a clue to that terrible day. And as we climbed on, higher and higher, and came out of the trees and on to open shrubland I felt suddenly freer and my anger began to ooze out of me like pus from a burst boil.

By the time we'd sighted Stammo's hut I'd completely recovered my senses. I told Paul that we ought to turn round and go down while there was still plenty of light but he replied that now we had come so far, we might as well say hello to Stammo first. Perhaps he still hoped for an explanation that would take the sting out of the awful feeling of disappointment that was gnawing inside him.

As we got near the hut we began to call. First we called Stammo, then Zak, then Stammo again, but we might as well have saved our breath for all the response we got. We pushed open the door of the hut and went in. It was empty but we noticed that the fire had only recently gone out; the ashes were still warm. A pot of half-cooked beans lay on its side on the floor and the old man's few possessions were strewn about the room as if he'd looked through them one by one and flung them to the ground. At the far end of the room the pots of yoghurt had fallen on to the flagstones and broken, the barrel of cheese had been overturned, the brine had all run out to form one huge stain on the floor and the cheese – there must have been fifty kilos in that barrel –

had been hacked into tiny, crumb-sized lumps. We left the hut and closed the door behind us.

Something wasn't right. It was still. Very still. Nothing stirred and there were none of the familiar sounds of a sheepfold – no sheep bleating, bells sounding or dogs barking, well, dog anyway. Zak! Where was Zak? He should have rounded the sheep up by now and led them into the pen. Perhaps they were already in, and Stammo was milking them.

The pen lay behind the hut, on a slope, and was not visible from where we were standing. Without knowing why, we began to run until we had the pen in sight. It looked abandoned, and even when we got much nearer we could see no movement or sign of activity – or life. But it was not until we pushed the rickety gate open and went right in that we finally found Stammo. He was lying amongst his animals, his high black boots pointing to the sky, his arms spread wide apart on either side of his body, his head strangely askew. We soon discovered that was because his throat had been slashed, and those of his sheep too. Only Zak seemed to have escaped. He sat by his master's side, whimpering sadly, his tail brushing the ground in a slow, mournful kind of way. We tried to take him with us when we left but he wouldn't budge from the old man's side. He looked so sad and so forlorn. A friend mourning the loss of a friend. It broke my heart to see him, and I thought it must be hard to be left behind like that.

Chapter Nineteen

We didn't go to the hills again after that. Poor Stammo was buried in the little cemetery beyond Notta the Herb-picker's house and the whole village turned out to pay their last respects. It seemed that everyone had been fond of the old man, but even so he had been brutally murdered. You must suspect all and no one: friends, neighbours, people you've known all your life, my father had told us . . . I looked around at the serious faces of the mourners. How does one go about suspecting a particular person, or persons? That sort of thing was for the police. They too were by the grave. Our Chief of Police with his stuck-up wife and revolting brat. Only I don't believe that they had come to mourn old Stammo or to offer their condolences to his family.

No one knew that it was Paul and I who had discovered Stammo. We made it home a little after dark and Grandmother, who'd been waiting for us out on the road, was ready to tear strips off us, but one look at our faces made her swallow her hard words and she led us into the house and listened in silence while we poured out our grief and our panic to her. 'You had a lucky escape,' she said gravely. 'Had whoever killed

Stammo still been there when you found his . . .' We nodded. Now that we were safe again we could see just how badly it could have turned out for us.

'I wish Mother had come,' said Paul softly.

Grandmother stroked his cheek. 'You know she would have done if it had been at all possible, don't you?' He nodded and bit his lip. In many ways he was still such a little boy.

Later, when we'd gone upstairs and were getting ready for bed, we asked Grandmother something that had been on our minds since we'd set off for the cave that morning.

'Grandmother . . .' I began.

'What is it, my dove?'

'How did you know where we were going this morning?'

She gave us a look full of mischief. 'The cheese, of course,' she said. 'Didn't you guess?'

And then I remembered the Sunday before when we'd come upon the men hiding in the cave, and how the wounded man had asked if he could have some of the cheese, and that one of the others, Andreas, had given it back to us only after we'd gone out of the cave.

'Is that how messages were passed around,' I exclaimed, 'inside the cheese?'

Grandmother nodded. 'It was clever,' she said, 'and it was Stammo who thought it up. That's why he didn't come to live in the village after his wife died. He stayed on at the *stani* to help us.'

'And someone betrayed him.'

'Yes, my children. Someone betrayed him but

whatever Stammo knew he took it with him. You can be sure of that.'

'He was a fine old man, Grandmother.'

'He was that, my boy . . . he was that.'

Then, before we went to our separate rooms, we told Grandmother we were sorry that we had lied to her and she said she was very sorry to have exposed us to all that danger, yet not trusted us enough to let us know what was going on. She said that circumstances had made some lies necessary but that there wouldn't be any more in future. When she kissed us goodnight she looked very merry and it was nice to feel that things were all right between us again.

Chapter Twenty

The riddle of the chickens that wouldn't lay was solved once and for all on April Fool's day. Spring had come and the Devil was in us, children and adults alike. The longer, warmer days, the air, light and caressing but also crystal clear and full of mischief, pushed itself into our heads and swept our minds clean of all traces of winter. Suddenly we felt lighter than a balloon, swifter than a lark, hungrier than a wolf, and with more energy than we knew what to do with.

Our grandmother, who never slept much anyway, slept even less now. On April Fool's Day she got up earlier than was usual even for her, while it was still dark outside. Well, there was nothing she could do that early in the morning without waking up the rest of us, so she decided to go outside, and when she'd done that she got the idea that she'd pay the hen-house a visit. Ritzo had suggested that there was nothing wrong with the hens. They did lay, he said, but something got to the eggs as soon as they were laid and that's why we never had more than a handful each day. Often there would be none at all. Anyway, Grandmother decided to give them the benefit of the doubt before marking them for the pot.

The birds were still roosting when she got to the hen-house, so she made herself comfortable behind the end wall and sat down to wait for the egg-thief. Grandmother couldn't be seen from the house but she herself had a clear view of it because the old planks were full of peep-holes. She didn't expect that anyone would come out of the house but it was good to be able to see it. Dawn broke and orchard, sea and sky were suddenly flooded by the rays of the rising sun, turning from grey to red and then to pink. A new day had begun.

Our grandmother was caught up in the wonder of it all, when she heard the noise of a door opening and closing in the house. It was a very soft, muted sound and only an old fox like Grandmother could have heard it. At first she thought it must be Aunt Hercules getting up but when she put her eye to one of the many holes in the planks she saw Marko walking towards the hen-house. Curious as to what had got him up so early, she didn't call out but kept her eyes firmly against the peep-hole to see what he was up to. Marko looked as if he didn't have a care in the world but when he came to the door of the hen-house he stopped and looked over his shoulder, as if to make sure that there was no one else about. Then he opened the door and went inside, shutting it behind him . . .

Grandmother couldn't make head or tail of it. What was Marko up to? One by one the chickens began to come out. They flapped their wings and stretched their necks and pranced around the way chickens do. And then, when they'd done that for a while, they began to cackle. First one, then another, then all of them together. And that's when Grandmother finally discovered why it was that, in spite of the very expensive corn she fed the hens, we hardly ever got any eggs from them. Marko followed the hens and picked up each egg as it dropped to the ground. When he had as many as he could carry, he left the hen-house with the still-warm eggs and made his way down to the eucalyptus tree at the end of the garden.

Grandmother left her hiding-place and began to follow him from a safe distance and soon she saw just what made Marko glow. Leaning against the massive trunk of one of the big trees, our cousin got down to breakfast. Making a hole at the top of each egg he put it to his mouth, closed his lips around the warm shell and sucked. When he'd finished, he gathered all the empty shells from the morning's crop of eggs and dropped them into a hole in the ground which he dug with a trowel he had brought with him. He had just begun to cover up the evidence when Grandmother, incensed by the sheer cheek of the crime, hurled herself at him shrieking like a thousand Furies.

Marko was paralysed ... rooted to the spot. Grabbing him by the hair, Grandmother broke off a length of eucalyptus branch, stripped the leaves off it and let it dance over poor Marko's thighs and bottom. 'There's an Italian proverb that says big mouthfuls often choke,' she shrieked at him, unmoved by his howls, prayers for mercy and promises that he would never do such a thing again. 'You've had your mouthful, my boy, now let's see you choke on it.'

Our greedy cousin was then dragged up the path to

the house, kicking and screaming fit to burst, but it didn't stop him getting a second beating, this time by his mother. 'May the Lord make my hands wither and drop off if I give you anything but bread and water from now on,' she panted, exhausted from the effort of holding Marko while she beat him. 'You are a thief and will be treated like one.' And she was as good as her word. Marko would have spent a lean Easter if Grandmother hadn't taken pity on him and persuaded Aunt Hercules to break her vow.

Holy Week began. On Maundy Thursday we went to communion taking a very reluctant Marko with us. The church was packed and the queue of people waiting to receive communion was so long that it spilt out on to the square and round the church itself. After what seemed like an age it was finally our turn. First Paul, then I, then . . . Marko's voice, clear as a bell, dropped a bombshell that shook the foundations of our little church. He was right in front of Pappa Michael but, instead of opening his mouth to receive the body and blood of Jesus, he was pointing with a trembling finger at the ikon of the Lord, the one in which he is seen blessing the little children. 'You hypocrite,' he screamed at the ikon, 'it was you who betrayed me . . . you . . . you . . . communist!'

The silence that followed was total, so complete that one could have heard a speck of dust hit the floor. But it didn't last long. Once people had recovered from their astonishment, a roar went up and soon there wasn't a dry eye to be seen. People were crying, not from sympathy with the suffering Christ, but with laughter. Never, never had anything like this happened in our church before and people simply couldn't stop laughing. Marko would have run out if Paul and I had not jumped on him and pinned his arms behind his back and forced the bread and the wine between his tightly closed lips. But though we'd made him take it we couldn't force him to swallow it, and as soon as we were outside he again showed just what he thought of Jesus by spitting out both the body and the blood of Our Lord.

Chapter Twenty-one

On Good Friday we followed the Epitafio, the coffin of Christ, when it was carried through the village, past houses where people were too sick or too old to join in the procession, along the edge of the sea, up to the square and finally back to the church.

Marko didn't come with us. He said he'd had enough of Jesus, apart from which he still hadn't forgiven Him for betraying him. Marko was still convinced that it was Jesus who had pointed Grandmother in the direction of the hen-house that fateful morning when she had caught him red-handed. But we wouldn't have missed the event for the world. It was lovely, magical. The long procession snaking through the narrow alleys of the village, the buzz of voices, the smell of the flowers strewn over the 'body' of Christ in his open coffin mingling with the smell of hundreds of yellow tapers, the monotonous chant of the priest and the shouts of 'Kyrie Eleison' by the choir boys, one of whom, believe it or not, was Aristo.

We went home once we'd seen the Epitafio safely back in church, but Aunt Hercules and Grandmother stayed on to hear the last Gospel. They weren't religious fanatics or anything like that but their lives were so hard that Holy Week and all that went with it was a bright spot in a series of dull and bitter days.

At last it was Easter Sunday. We shouted, 'Christ has risen', and hugged and kissed one another before we threw ourselves on the basket of dyed eggs. Not Marko though. He seemed to have gone off eggs. Later, when Grandmother was sure that we hadn't given ourselves indigestion from all the hard-boiled eggs we'd eaten, she gave us the other Easter eggs – the ones filled with sweets. Marko got one, too, though his mother didn't want him to have one. She said that he didn't deserve such a treat, but Grandmother said that she thought Marko had learned his lesson; he had promised never to do anything so selfish again.

We stayed in the yard with Aki most of the morning, helping him to unwrap his sweets, playing with him and singing and dancing for him. He loved it when I danced. Of all the things we did to amuse him, watching me dance was what he liked best. As he watched me do leaps and turns and pirouettes, he would urge me on by clapping his poor limp hands together; his eyes would become two bright stars, the blood would rush to his cheeks, and for a while he would look as healthy and normal as any boy.

Eventually Aki fell asleep, and finding ourselves at a loose end we voted for rounding up the gang and going down to the square. We found most of the others at home and they were only too glad to join up with us. Easter Day, after the excitement of eggs and things had died down, was a dull kind of day and any suggestion for action was greeted with loud cheers. Well, we hadn't been there five minutes when Cyclops Jr. and his band of Warriors strutted on to the scene. We were standing on opposite sides of the square kind of sizing each other up when Aristo opened his ugly mouth and shouted: 'Hey you.' He meant me.

I made a show of looking behind me. 'No one there, Aristo,' I said.

'It's you I want, Antigone Laskari.'

'Oh, me. What can I do for you, baby?' It was a joy to see him blush.

'Over here,' he ordered.

'To hell with you, Aristo,' I shouted back. 'I don't take orders from anyone . . . especially not from a fascist like you.'

'You communist bitch,' he retorted.

He was feeding me what I needed to smash his face for him. 'You've got a mouth like a sewer, you know that.'

'Anything that comes out of it is too clean for you.'

'Watch she doesn't bite your other leg,' Gina called out insolently.

Aristo's eyes shot poisoned arrows at us. 'You wait, we'll get you . . . all of you, and exterminate you like the vermin you are.'

'Like you did old Stammo,' I shot at him softly, and something that had lain dangerously quiet inside me ever since Paul and I had found the old man suddenly uncoiled and rose up in me. I went up to Aristo and my hand went back in a wide arc over my shoulder and sprang back of its own accord, catching Aristo on the right side of the face and knocking him off his feet. He picked himself up quickly enough but a thin stream of blood began to trickle from his nose to his upper lip, down his chin and on to the lapel of his dazzling white jacket.

'I'll make you pay for this, you see if I don't. Every one of you red bastards will pay for it,' he yelled, his voice high and shrill like a girl's.

I had to think fast. Grandmother had warned me against getting into any more fights with Aristo and now I had. However . . . 'Listen,' I told him, 'how about you and me having a fight . . .' (if he was as vain as I'd heard he was . . .) 'with . . . kites.'

He threw his head back and roared with laughter. 'You . . . fight me . . . a kite-fight with a girl . . . Any time.' He'd swallowed it hook, line and sinker.

'Right,' I said demurely. 'Will tomorrow do you?'

'Suits me,' he replied, nearly wetting himself he was having so much fun. But of course he couldn't leave it at that. 'After tomorrow you'll wish you'd never been born,' he bragged.

'The loudest drum has nothing but air in it,' I replied sweetly, satisfied with the worried looks that had come over the ugly mugs of Aristo's hooligans. They knew something he didn't and it was doubtful that he'd have listened to them even if they'd tried to tell him.

'Now,' said George, one of Ritzo's twins, 'if you can take Aristo's kite from him . . .'

'Nothing to it,' I mocked, 'only, to take Aristo's kite from him with the whole village watching is like asking to be beaten to death.'

'We have Paul,' piped up Lou-Lou.

And having Paul was something in our favour because though he looked like an angel with his large eyes and soft brown curls, he was an expert marksman. No one flung a stone as surely as Paul with his left arm.

'Yes,' I said, 'Aristo might not know of it, but his guerrillas do, and they'll make themselves scarce around him.' I looked at my brother. 'If it comes to a fight you'll be the one in the front line, you know that, don't you?'

Paul nodded. 'Don't worry about me, you just keep the ammunition coming.'

'You bet.'

'What kite are you going to use?' asked the other twin.

'The "Lark",' I answered.

Louka laughed. 'You know, I almost feel sorry for Aristo. He just doesn't know what's going to hit him.'

'Save your sympathy,' said Gina. 'If Andi does take his kite, he and his hooligans will be after us to slit our throats.'

'But not before I've brained them all,' retorted Paul.

'Remember old Stammo,' I whispered to him.

A shiver ran through Paul. He didn't say much after that and (in a way) I was sorry I'd reminded him of it.

Paul and I had lots of kites but the biggest and the best was the 'Lark'. It was made of newspaper and lined with the gauze that grandmother used for cheese-making. Our father had taught us to make them like that years ago and we'd gone on making them this way ever since. Ours were solid and well-balanced and, though it sounds like boasting, I still say that no one could make kites like we did and no one could beat me at kite-flying. To be a good kite-fighter it makes no difference whether one is a boy or a girl. The important thing is to have strong, agile arms and to know how to get the string off your opponent, because if you can do that you can capture his kite at the same time. That's what I had to do tomorrow. Get Aristo's string and take his kite away from him. Sounds easy, doesn't it?

Chapter Twenty-two

Easter Monday was a lovely day with clear skies and warm, balmy winds, soft as kisses. We were the first to arrive at the square. I released my kite and at once it soared upward, trailing its twenty-odd metres of tail behind it.

The news of the fight had spread like fire through the village and people came to their doors and balconies to watch. They'd seen me at kite-flying before but this was special. Cassandra's and Antony's 'orphans' had challenged the son of the most dangerous and powerful man in the village to a kite-fight and they wouldn't have missed it for anything.

I squinted up at the 'Lark' but all was well. There was no 'belly' in the string; no chance of it falling out of the sky for lack of tail. On the whole the 'Lark' was very well-behaved. I'd already warmed up nicely when Aristo marched into the square with his thugs in tow. He too sent his kite up, a splendid red, yellow and blue affair, but I saw at once that, impressive though it might look, it was not a kite made for serious flying. It didn't have enough tail. In short, the 'Athenian' was no real threat to my 'Lark'. Aristo had a bull-roarer on his and it made an awful racket. No doubt it made Aristo feel important, but bull-roarer or not, his kite was not responding well to his tugging and pulling and for a while it looked as if it would plunge back to earth.

'Hey Aristo,' someone called, 'watch out Andi doesn't take your kite off you.'

'We'll see,' snarled Aristo, frantically trying to get his kite into some kind of order.

And when at last the kite-battle began it went my way right from the start. Aristo's string 'bellied', then 'mouthed' too much forward and was constantly threatening to come spinning down. I was not surprised. I had expected it ever since I'd seen his tail. The 'Lark', on the other hand, her string taut as steel, hung perfectly still, like a sun, and I had twenty-five metres of string ready to be fed from my hand to the sky.

'Bravo,' people called, 'Bravo Andi', and 'You might as well give her your kite now, Aristo, she'll take it anyway.'

I swelled with pride then. It was now or never. 'Aristo,' I shouted, 'are you ready?'

'To hell with you,' was all I got back.

I began the manoeuvre of 'close approach' and set my trap. Aristo, who knew as little about flying kites as he did about everything else, fell into it. I lost no time in placing myself on his string, forcing him to 'crush' me. Putting more weight on his kite, which was too heavy already, Aristo began to pull but he hadn't noticed that I wasn't making mine 'belly'. I still held my string taut as steel. While he pulled, I relaxed. Then he pulled more strongly, bumping me. I began loosening my kite and

kept on loosening her, and when Aristo reached the top
I took to moving mine off from left to right and back
again, forkwise.

'Pull,' I shouted to the gang. 'Pull hard before he gets
to unwind.' He saw what we were about but much too
late. The 'Lark' had Aristo's proud 'Athenian' by the
throat. The crowd went wild. 'She's got you now,
Aristo. Andi's got you now. Your fancy "Athenian" can
kiss her tail.'

Unseen by any of us, two of Aristo's thugs had drawn
their 'cut-throats', ready to cut my string as the 'Lark'
began to come down. But Paul knew his stuff. Using
stones no bigger than walnuts, he aimed, got them right
between the eyes and sent them packing.

'Pull,' I yelled again. 'Pull, everyone pull.' And they
all did. Even little Aleko whose pants slid down to his
ankles every time he jumped up to meet the string.

Then, crash! and the two kites came down like mill-
stones, skimming over the roof of the church, taking
half the tiles with them. Aristo's string snapped and
kites, cords and tails came tumbling over us.

'Look out!' someone screamed. 'Look out, Andi.
They're coming after you with cut-throats.'

I had expected some kind of battle but I had not
expected them to go after us with knives. I pushed my
'Lark' and Aristo's 'Athenian' at the twins and
screamed at them to make themselves scarce. Then I
joined the others to help gather ammunition. Walking
backwards, always backwards, we swept the street
clean of stones, piling them into little pyramids for Paul
to find as he covered our retreat. With a constant supply

of fresh ammunition he cracked the heads of half-a-dozen of the enemy in the first five minutes. But they still came, their faces streaked with blood, determined to 'mark' at least some of us with their knives.

In the end, thanks to Paul's brilliant marksmanship, they began to fall back, becoming smaller and smaller as we put more and more road between them and ourselves. But we kept on walking backwards, stones at the ready, until we felt the gate of Grandmother's house at our backs. I carried the 'Athenian' upstairs and hung it on the wall above my and Grandmother's bed. She was very angry with me for having broken my promise not to fight Aristo. She even tried to make me return the 'Athenian'.

'I can't do that, Grandmother, it was a fair fight and I won. The kite belongs to me now.'

'I still think you should give it back.'

'I won't,' I replied defiantly.

'I don't know what's got into you,' she said wearily. 'You've become so wild lately.'

I pulled the blankets over my head and bit the inside of my mouth to stop myself from crying. Why is it that good days always end up bad?

Chapter Twenty-three

You know how sometimes you can 'see' something though it is not there? That's what happened to me the night after the kite-fight. Tired out by the long day, and with my arms aching from pulling the kite, I fell asleep quickly. I don't know what time it was or how long I had been asleep when I 'saw' someone standing by my bed.

'Grandmother,' I murmured, and felt for her beside me, but the space next to me was empty and cold. I rolled on to my back and drifted back to sleep and dreamed that my mother was bending over me, stroking my hair and tucking the bedclothes around me. She was wearing her partisan uniform with the red cross stitched into the lapels and on the shoulder tabs of the jacket. Her long hair was tied back, away from her face, her eyes, so like Paul's, were calm and still, her lips slightly apart as if she was about to speak.

'Mother,' I whispered, trying hard to push the weight off my eyes.

'Andi, my darling, my precious little girl.'

'Oh Mother,' I cried, 'we waited and waited for you but you didn't come. Oh, Mother, we were so unhappy.'

'Shh . . . my baby. I am here now.'

'Stay with us, Mother. Please say you'll stay.'

She looked sad then and suddenly she was gone and I woke up and screamed and Grandmother came running upstairs and took me in her arms and rocked me like a baby and I sobbed and sobbed until there were no more tears left in me.

I was ill for a while after that. Well, not ill exactly. I didn't have a temperature or anything like that but Grandmother said I might as well stay home for a few days. Paul and Marko kept me up-to-date with reports on what was going on 'outside'.

'Cyclops Jr. is in an ugly mood,' Paul said one day. 'He's sworn to get you for taking his kite.'

'I didn't take it, I won it. It was a fair fight.'

'He doesn't know what "fair" means,' said Marko darkly.

'You're right there,' I replied, 'but in any case what can he do? He'll forget about it once school starts.'

'I don't think people like Aristo ever forget anything,' said Paul slowly, his beautiful eyes dark and troubled. 'And he's got really creepy lately. He and his louts have taken to sneaking up on Marko and me at all sorts of times. It's like he was stalking us.'

Marko thought that was very funny. Roaring like a tiger, he sprang at Paul, knocking him to the floor. But Paul's mind was not on playing games. 'Lay off, will you,' he shouted and threw Marko off him.

'All right, all right,' Marko sulked.

I ran my hands through my brother's hair. 'Don't worry, angel,' I told him, realizing that I sounded like

Mother had done in my dream. 'He wouldn't dare touch you. He knows I'd pull out his whiskers one by one if he tried.'

'But what if you are not there to do it? What then?' asked my brother softly.

I didn't reply and they went. I was relieved and worried all at the same time, but glad to be alone again. Boy, did they depress me.

Chapter Twenty-four

Aunt Dina suddenly decided that she and the boys would come and spend a few days with us after all, but apart fom saying hello and all that, I didn't see much of them. I preferred to be on my own most of the time, just then, and I found it hard to look at Aunt Dina without becoming really miserable. She looked so like Mother that just being near her gave me a headache. Then Grandmother would take me upstairs and put cold compresses on my forehead and sometimes she'd stay with me until I'd fallen asleep.

Once when she'd gone back down, I heard them discussing me. 'You are spoiling that girl,' Aunt Dina said. 'Sitting up there by herself all day. At least make her open her books. She ought to be revising with the exams only weeks away.' Then she said something which really made me sit up. 'Not that there's any real point, I suppose,' she went on. 'They'll fail her however well she does.'

'Don't say that,' Grandmother protested. 'To the examining board she'll only be one more child . . .'

'That just shows how much you know about it, Mother,' Aunt Dina retorted.

'We must still hope,' replied my wonderful grand-mother.

'Doesn't cost anything,' said Aunt Dina sarcastically, 'but I'm telling you she hasn't got a chance and it's all Cassie's fault for having let herself become tarred with the brush of communist ideologies.'

'You should know, having got it straight from the horse's mouth,' snapped Aunt Hercules.

Me, I wished that something awful would happen to Aunt Dina.

Chapter Twenty-five

And something awful did happen to our Aunt Dina. A few days after she'd left Uncle Tasso alone in Athens, to come to us, he, Uncle Tasso that is, had gone for his evening glass of ouzo to the Café Rosita just round the corner from where they lived. He'd stayed until ten o'clock, as usual, then he'd had one last ouzo, bought a new packet of cigarettes and left to go home. He'd just rounded the corner and must have been only about fifty yards from his front door when someone jumped on him and stuck a knife in his back. It seems that even the army couldn't take care of its own all of the time.

I had never liked Uncle Tasso, he'd been sly and false with a smile that had never gone further than the corners of his mouth, but I was sorry that he was dead. We might have been friends, perhaps, if only there hadn't been a war on.

And so we got to know our Athenian cousins better because after their father was killed they did not go back to Athens. We liked the younger boys, Mano, Theodor and little Niko, who was only four years old, but we didn't like Mitso, the oldest boy. He was very like his father, both to look at and in his ways. His eyes, for instance, would rove over everything and everyone whenever he came into a room and he always homed in on every sound and whisper inside the house and out of it. I tell you, he gave Marko, Paul and me the creeps.

And what a temper he had. One day he demanded to be allowed to fly the 'Lark'. I said I never lent the 'Lark' to anyone, not even to Paul or Marko, but that I'd show him how to make a kite and then he could make one himself . . . Well, he went all white and rigid, as if about to have a fit or something, then he yelled that communists were supposed to share everything and he hated them because it was they who'd killed his father, but he'd get even with us and . . . He ranted on like that for a long time but I went up to my room and left him to it. Only now I knew we had a live bomb in the house.

I told Paul and Marko what had happened and all three of us tried to tell Grandmother but she said not to be silly. Mitso was only ten years old, the same age as Paul, and it wasn't easy for a boy suddenly to lose his father (who was she telling, we wondered) and that we must all make allowances for him.

Our cousins came to our school with us when it opened again, except little Niko who was too young, but he found a perfect playmate in Aki and for a while things went quite well.

Then, one day I spotted Mitso together with Aristo. I suppose it was inevitable that they should have got together, being on the same 'side' and all, but it got my gall to see someone from my family being friendly with Aristo. I called him over to me.

'What do you want?' he asked rudely.

I counted to ten, then took a deep breath. 'Listen, Mitso,' I said, 'you are welcome to join our gang if you want to. You don't have to hang about with them,' I thrust my chin towards Aristo and his louts. 'They are no good.'

'Who says?' he said, giving me plenty of cheek.

'I do.'

'Well, I don't agree with you. Aristo is my friend and I'll talk to him as much as I like. He is a Monarchist like my father was, not an ELLAS traitor like you and the rest at home and I hate you all and . . .'

'You hate too much,' I interrupted him, sick to death of his ranting.

'You just wait till someone gets your father,' he said.

Chapter Twenty-six

It was a grand spring. The swallows returned to build their nests under our roof, the sea lost its roughness and became a vast sheet of blue polished marble. No more grey clouds hung over the hills and a smile had appeared on the stony lips of the Sleeper. There was every kind of flower growing in the fields, the peach and the cherry were in bloom and on the almond trees tiny green fruits, soft and velvety to the touch, peaked out between the leaves. The tortoises ambled through the orchard looking like stones on legs; lizards darted in and out of the cracks in walls doing whatever lizards do; kids, only hours old, skipped after their mothers. Even the adder looked affectionate basking in the sun surrounded by its mass of wriggling young. There was life in everything, good and bad, ugly and beautiful. It was good to know that war had not been able to stop spring from coming.

I too felt fresh and full of energy and made up my mind to ignore what I'd heard Aunt Dina say about me. I worked like never before for the coming exams, now frighteningly close. I'd go straight home after school, grab a piece of bread, dip it in oil and gnaw on it while I worked. All in all, life was good again and filled with possibilities. Aunt Dina and her boys had slowly got used to our ways and even Mitso seemed to have lost some of his loathing for us. We didn't speak much and as long as we kept out of each other's way things were fine between us. Aunt Dina had joined forces with Aunt Hercules and between them they took to bossing us about something terrible.

It was all right for Marko and our Athenian cousins, their mothers had had every right to tell them what to do, but Paul and I resented it. Before, with only Aunt Hercules to cope with, it hadn't been so bad but now there were two mothers to order us about and neither of them was ours.

We came home from school one afternoon to find a yellow bicycle leaning against the gate. We stood a long time admiring it and taking bets as to whose it could be. There weren't many bicycles in the village and certainly none as fine as this one. In the yard there was no one to be seen except Aki and little Niko and they didn't seem to think that anything unusual might be going on.

'Anyone here, then?' Mitso asked his little brother.

'They are upstairs,' Niko replied, and went back to playing with Aki.

We looked up at the house. The window of the *sala* was open and peals of laughter from Aunt Dina and Aunt Hercules floated down to us. Moments later there was another burst of laughter, thicker and darker this time. It was a voice that we couldn't remember ever having heard before. We flung our school satchels in a heap on the ground and hoisted ourselves up on the wall, sitting in a straight line like sparrows on a tele-graph wire, straining our ears to catch even the faintest of sounds from the *sala*, rigid with suspense.

Ages later the door upstairs opened and Grand-mother came through it closely followed by a tall, thin man, not old and not young, with an enormous yellow moustache and sparkling black eyes as bright as a mag-pie's. After them came our two aunts trying hard to look dignified but giggling like a couple of schoolgirls. Having come down, they went to sit under the canopy of vines and Aunt Dina went into the house and came out with a bottle of ouzo and four glasses. There was some kind of speech, after which they drank to some-one's long life and happiness. Then Aunt Hercules, looking strangely flushed, said something about making coffee and hurried into the house. All this went on right in front of us yet no one was taking the slightest notice of us. It was as if we didn't exist.

After the coffee, they chatted on about this and that – mostly about the war and the high price of every-thing – and then the thin man got up to go. Only then did he glance at us, but mostly at Marko, and before he went out of the gate he patted Aki on the head as if he had been a dog or something. We waited till he was out on the road, then we scrabbled off the wall and poured out after him, before Grandmother could close the gate.

We were just in time to see the thin man before he disappeared round the bend. He was pedalling with-out holding on to the handlebars, his body swaying with the motion of the bicycle, all loose-limbed and fancy free, whistling a popular tune, with the easy, light-as-air-arrogance of an Athenian dandy.

'Grandmother,' I asked after we were in bed, 'who was the man that came here this afternoon?'

Grandmother, who'd been reading, closed her book and turned to me. 'He wants to marry your Aunt Hara,' she said with a glint in her eyes.

'Oh,' I let out, taken completely by surprise. 'Oh, Grandmother, how exciting, are you sure? Is he a good man?'

'I hope so. At any rate he seems prepared to take on her boys and be a father to them and few men are prepared to do something like that. Your aunt told him right from the beginning that there was nothing doing otherwise.'

'Do you think he's as easygoing as Aunt?' I said. Grandmother pretended to be cross at that but I think that she was only putting it on out of loyalty. After all, Aunt Hercules was her child.

'Your aunt isn't easygoing, Andi. She . . . she . . . well, she doesn't let things get her down, that's all.'

'What about Marko, has he been told yet?'

'I don't think so. It's too early for that.'

'What will she tell him?'

'I don't know, Andi, but I expect the moment will bring the right words.'

'Will Marko have to call him "father"?'

'I suppose so.'

'Poor Marko.' I shuddered, remembering everything I'd heard and read about step-parents.

Grandmother looked surprised. 'Why "poor Marko"? It will do him good to have a father. He is a boy who needs to have a man around.'

'When will they get married?'

'Not for a while yet. It wouldn't be respectful to Aunt Dina to seem too eager about it.'

Grandmother went back to her book and I snuggled up close to her, to the warmth and safety of her broad back which had been like a wall between me and everything that was bad and ugly and false all my life.

'Goodnight, Grandmother,' I murmured.

'Goodnight, Andi.'

'Grandmother . . .'

'Yes.'

'I hope Aunt Hercules and Marko and Aki will be happy when they go to live with the thin man.'

'I hope so too, my dove.'

'Goodnight, Grandmother.'

'Goodnight, my girl.'

Chapter Twenty-seven

One evening when I was at my homework upstairs, there was a knock on the gate doors. It was a carefully measured knock, loud enough to be heard but not loud enough to attract undue attention. I went over to one of the windows facing the road and in the light from the street lamp I saw that it was the schoolmaster.

Mitso opened the gate to him and they went inside. Soon I heard them all talking and laughing and Aunt Dina asking in that high voice of hers about her boys and how they were getting on and the schoolmaster answering in a voice that was much too loud and much too jolly that they were doing fine. They were all of them fine boys and she could be proud of them. Then Aunt Dina cried a little and mumbled something about how difficult it was to bring up four lively boys without a father. The schoolmaster answered yes, it was sad, but that we lived in sad times. After a bit more of the same stuff, he wished them goodnight and he and Grandmother came out together to the gate. As he went through the great doors, I saw him push something into Grandmother's hand. She put whatever it was into the pocket of her apron, and locked up.

Later, when she came to bed, I pretended to be asleep. She undressed quickly and after she'd put on her nightdress she pulled the thing out of her apron. It was a letter. I only got a quick look at it but from what I saw, I was sure that it was from abroad.

Grandmother sat down on the edge of the bed and, snatching a pin out of her hair, she put it under the flap of the envelope and slit it open. Then she began to read. She caught her breath several times while she was reading and when she'd finished it she went back to the beginning and read it all over again. She did that twice more as if she needed to convince herself that the contents would be the same each time, before folding it up and fitting it back into the envelope. That done, she began to look around the room, going over it inch by inch the way one does when one wants to make sure that one is really alone. Having satisfied herself that there was nothing in our room that shouldn't be there, she lifted the mattress and pushed the letter under it.

Chapter Twenty-eight

The visit by the schoolmaster was followed by one from Old Cyclops, our Chief of Police. He stole into our house quietly, like a thief for whom the door had been left on the latch. We neither saw nor heard him or his 'boys' until they let loose with their boots on the upstairs door. Grandmother, afraid that they'd kick the door in, got up to open it, but they were in before she reached the hall and, pushing her before them, they forced their way into our room.

One by one everyone in the house woke up and came to our room to see what was going on. Aunt Dina, Aunt Hercules, Marko and Manos. The only one not there was Mitso, but no one thought much of it at the time. We had our hands full looking after ourselves. The Chief of Police, made nervous by the presence of so many people, shouted for silence. He had two other policemen with him. One was Vassili, whom we'd known for years, and the other was Jan, a nephew of Ritzo's. Ritzo often said how sorry he was that Jan should have chosen to join the police.

Old Cyclops looked us over for a while, then he held out his hand to Aunt Dina. 'My condolences on the tragic death of your husband, madame,' he said, clicking his heels together the way the Germans had done.

'Thank you,' Aunt Dina mumbled, withdrawing her hand as soon as it was decent to do so. I got the feeling that Old Cyclops's condolences had been an embarrassment rather than a comfort to her. Uncle Tasso might have been a Monarchist, but that didn't mean that she looked on the police as bosom pals. Besides, Uncle Tasso had only been a cadet when they'd married.

Grandmother always said that war brings out the best and the worst in people, and one didn't have to be a genius to see what she meant. Perhaps the Chief of Police too would have been a nice man if he'd been just an ordinary Chief of Police in ordinary times. The war gave him plenty of excuses to behave badly and he used them all. He was that kind of person. And now that he had got everyone out of bed, he ordered them all downstairs, except for Grandmother, Paul and me. We were told to stay behind. He ordered Vassili to go with them but kept Jan to help look after us.

When they'd all gone, he said in a voice that made it very clear that he would not tolerate any contradictions: 'I have the questions and I happen to know you have the answers. And I want them. Now.'

No one spoke.

'Well, did the cat get your tongues?'

The silence deepened. Old Cyclops began to flex his fingers. He pointed to me. 'You,' he said, 'when did you last see your father?'

'I haven't seen him.'

He kept his head moving all the time, from me to

116

Grandmother, from her to Paul and back again, searching our faces for clues. He turned to Paul. 'And you, when did you see him last?'

'I don't know, but it must have been a long time ago, because I can't even remember what he looks like,' answered Paul cleverly, and I forgave him the exaggeration, as Father too would have done.

After us, it was Grandmother's turn. 'Well, Mrs Andippa, if the children haven't seen their father, perhaps you have heard something from him?' He was looking much more dangerous now.

'I'm afraid I can't help you,' Grandmother said quietly, as if they had been discussing the whereabouts of an old acquaintance. 'It's like the children told you, their father hasn't been here lately.'

'And you swear that you haven't heard from him either?'

'Yes.'

He leaned forward on his feet. There was a glint of metal in his hand and all of a sudden Grandmother was lying on the floor with an ugly, angry gash across her forehead. It began to bleed immediately. The blood ran over her eyes, across the bridge of her nose, down her chin and on to the floor.

'Grandmother,' we screamed and threw ourselves over her to keep her from being hit again. I looked up at Jan.

'Stop him,' I pleaded. 'Please stop him, don't let him touch her again.'

'Let her be,' roared Cyclops.

But something happened to Jan. A look of disgust

washed over his face and he swept past Old Cyclops and then he was bending over Grandmother, wiping the blood off her face with his handkerchief as gently as if she'd been his own mother. 'Don't worry, Auntie,' he said. 'Don't you worry, everything is going to be all right.' And then I thought how proud Ritzo would be if he could see Jan now and how Jan was a chip off the old block after all.

'Thank you, my boy,' said Grandmother. 'God will reward you for your kindness.'

Jan almost cried then. 'I'm sorry, Auntie,' he whispered. 'I didn't know, I never thought . . .'

'Poor Jan,' replied Grandmother softly. 'To make a good policeman in these dark times you must first learn to frighten children and knock down old women. Then, when you've learned that, they might let you shoot someone.'

That got Cyclops going again. 'Against the wall, all of you,' he roared.

Jan put his arms around Grandmother and pulled her to her feet. She'd turned yellow like a candle and I am sure that she would have fallen again had Jan not kept his arms about her. I pulled up a chair and he lowered her on to it. Paul went to stand by her, and that only left me still against the wall.

'Put your hands up.'

I put my hands over my head. He began to pace up and down in front of me, then he stopped, and bored his good eye into me. 'I repeat, where's your father?'

A new silence followed and it was while I was looking into his eye that I suddenly saw him as he was, a little

118

man with a peaked hat much too big for him, and then I remembered that thing that Grandmother had told me about fear. I thought, yes, it's true, he doesn't really scare me, what scares me is thinking about being scared, and I felt myself smiling and Jan smiled and I'm sure he would have got it from Old Cyclops if he'd seen it, but Jan was careful to keep his smile safe so that it wouldn't hurt any of us.

'Well, do I get an answer or not?' It was funny how much like a schoolmaster he sounded. Perhaps those who couldn't make it to become schoolmasters got to become policemen instead.

'I really haven't seen my father,' I replied. 'None of us have. It's like my brother told you. It's so long since we saw him that we've even forgotten what he looks like.'

He stopped pacing up and down. Instead he pushed the gun against my chest. 'I see. So you've neither seen him nor heard from him. Of course, in that case you don't know that a man was found drifting in a small boat just outside the harbour of Alexandria and that he was caught by the authorities there and put in prison.' He was so close to me then that I could feel his foul breath on my face. He smelled really bad, as if everything inside him was rotten. 'By the way, the name of the boat was *The Little Nutshell*,' he said, his eyes riveted on my face.

It was at that point that I began to laugh because suddenly I understood so much of what had been happening lately. I knew now what the schoolmaster had slipped Grandmother as he was leaving. I laughed like a drain. I laughed until the tears were running down my face. I laughed as if I'd been at a Punch and Judy show. 'Tom Thumb,' I cried, 'was a little boy. He was only as big as my thumb or as big as a man with a lot of sea around him and he sailed away in the night to get away from the ugly toad who wanted to put him in prison.'

Old Cyclops looked murderous. A black cloud had settled on his peaked cap and I was sure that he was going to pull the trigger, but I didn't care. All I could think of was that Father had made it. He'd sailed across the Aegean and he had had God knows what adventures. He'd been captured and escaped and now he was safe and well in some far-off country and had written to let us know. Who wouldn't have laughed at something like that!

Old Cyclops didn't think it was funny. His hand caught me across the face and my head jerked back and hit the wall behind me and for a few moments there seemed to be ten of us in the room instead of five. But I have a hard head and soon I had the room in focus again. But I did stop laughing. I'd laughed all I needed to. Cyclops had had all he could take and made ready to leave, followed by Jan. But he just had to have the last word. 'Don't think I've done with you,' he said darkly.

And at last he went, and my legs began to shake and the next moment they'd buckled under me and before I knew it I lay on the floor bathed in cold sweat, shivering all over and as weak as if I'd had the flu. But it didn't last long and when I'd recovered I was as bubbly as a brook inside. I threw my arms around Paul and Grandmother and held them tight and I told Paul about Father being safe, and promised him that everything was going to be all right.

And Paul said yes, he was glad, of course he was glad for Father, and then he brought me down in mid-flight like he might have brought down a swallow with a single shot from his sling by asking, ever so gently: 'And Mother. What about her? Is she safe too?'

Chapter Twenty-nine

A couple of evenings later Ritzo came and took Grand-mother aside and told her to get us all out of the house because he'd heard from Jan (who'd lost no time in leaving the police force but had to serve a term for insubordination before they would let him go) that 'they' were talking of burning down our house. Ritzo offered to take us, but Grandmother said that as the nights were warm enough for us sleep out, we'd camp in the orchard for a few days. Everyone except Mitzo thought it would be fun. He moaned and groaned about how uncomfort-able it was to have to sleep on the ground and in the end his mother told him that if he didn't like it he could go and sleep in the house by himself and that shut him up.

After a couple of nights of sleeping under the trees, we returned to sleep in the house again. Aunt Hercules said she'd had enough and would take her chances with 'them' rather than spend another night under a tree. She had no time for either partisans or Monarchists – or politics, for that matter. She loved my parents but thought them crazy and irresponsible. She said being a grass widow had not been her choice but our parents had chosen to make Paul and me grass orphans and that it was wrong however one looked at it. She and Aunt Dina talked like that a lot. Paul said it was lucky for us that the thin man had come along because now that they had other things to talk about, they might leave off slugging our parents.

One evening when, as usual, I'd gone upstairs to be alone, I heard Aunt Dina say that once the 'troubles' were over she'd go back to Athens. It was nice in the village but she'd got used to life in Athens and missed it. I thought Aunt Hercules would protest but she didn't. Instead, she said that in that case she'd ask Savva, the thin man, if he minded moving in with her and her boys, here, in Grandmother's house, instead of them going to live with him in Piraeus. That way, when Grandmother was no longer able to look after herself, there'd be someone to take care of her.

Grandmother laughed at that. I bet she didn't see herself as ever needing to be looked after. At any rate not by Aunt Hercules, who was both kind and clever in her own way but who 'drank the coffee but didn't wash the cup'. 'Thank you, daughter,' she said, 'but once you and Savva take over the house I'll get nothing but the inside of the olive and the outside of the walnut.'

'Oh, Mother. How you talk. Savva really likes you.'

'Everyone likes the mother of the bride, child, but a mother-in-law in the house is something entirely different,' Grandmother replied kindly. 'But you are welcome to stay on here with Savva, if that's what you want.' I don't know but I suspect that they were both thinking of the last time that Aunt Hercules had left to follow a husband.

A while later I heard Aunt Hercules ask the boys to take a bottle and go to Anna's for retsina.* Paul came up to ask if I wanted to go with them but I told him I didn't feel like it and went back to my books. Then I must have dozed off because the next thing I heard was a lot of screaming and shouting, people running, doors and windows opening and closing. A mob seemed to have gathered out there. An angry, loud, undisciplined, excited mob, and it was coming towards our house. I ran over to the window to see if I could make out what was going on but it was too dark to see properly and, needing to stretch my legs, I decided to go and see for myself.

I raced down the stairs and across the yard, flung open the gate and ran straight into Uncle Savva, as we already called him, just as he was coming through with Paul in his arms – a pale, limp, lifeless Paul, drained of blood and floppy as a rag doll. I threw myself at Savva, wanting to take Paul from him, only someone grabbed me and pinned me against the gate so that Savva could pass. But if I couldn't move, I could scream, and I yelled and yelled, crying and pleading to be set free all at the same time and at last Grandmother came and took me in to see my brother.

They'd put him on Aunt Hercules's bed and had piled every blanket in the house on top of him, and buried under that mound of covers he looked so small and still and white that I just knew that he would not move again. I put my face on his and kissed his closed

*A Greek wine flavoured with resin.

eyes, the white mouth and the baby-soft curls. He had wanted them cut off but Mother had made him promise not to – not till she was home again.

I clutched at Grandmother's hand, forcing her on to the bed with me and Paul. 'He is going to be all right, isn't he, Grandmother?' She kissed me. 'Let's hope so, my dove, let's hope so.'

Then the doctor came and after he'd examined Paul he said that he'd had quite a blow to the back of the head and that the next forty-eight hours would be critical.

'May we move him upstairs, doctor?' Grandmother asked.

'Yes, but be careful not to make any sudden movements while carrying him and then don't move him again.'

'How long is he going to be like this?' It was Aunt Dina who'd asked.

The doctor sighed. 'Not easy to say. He could wake up now, tonight, tomorrow . . . he . . .' There he suddenly stopped, but I knew he'd been about to say 'never' and I thought how much I would have hated him if he had. As he was leaving, the doctor asked: 'How did it happen?'

Mitso, who'd just come in through the door, tried to leave again when he caught sight of Paul on the bed, but I'd seen him and flung myself after him and grabbed him before he could get away. I had him by the shoulders and I shook him till his teeth began to rattle. 'Ask him,' I shouted, 'ask him.'

Aunt Dina flew at me like a tigress. 'Let go of him,

you crazy girl,' she yelled. 'Whatever makes you think he had anything to do with it?'

'Because he is like his father,' I yelled back, hardly knowing what I was saying.

'You're crazy,' joined in Mitso, cocky now that his mother was there to defend him. 'You're crazy. I was nowhere near him,' he pointed at the still figure on the bed, 'I was with . . .' and that's where he stopped, but it didn't matter. I knew where he'd been and he knew I did.

'Say it,' I screamed at him, 'say it if you dare. Say, "I betrayed Paul. I saw him and my brothers and Marko go to Anna's but Andi wasn't with them and I thought now is the time to teach him a lesson he will not forget and so I ran and told Aristo and he set the Warriors on them. After roughing the others up a bit they were to concentrate on Paul." Come on, Mitso, say it, say, "I knew what they were going to do but I didn't try to stop them, I wanted them to kill Paul." Say it.'

Mitso had gone as white as Paul. 'You are crazy,' he said, 'everyone knows you are crazy.'

'Better crazy than a police stooge,' I shouted and when he hit out at me I spat in his face.

Aunt Dina would have hit me herself had Grandmother not stopped her. 'Leave her alone,' she said. 'Can't you see that she is suffering?'

Marko, his arms and face covered in bruises, pushed his way through the crowd of people in the room and put his arms around me and soon we were both of us crying because though he was greedy and tight-fisted he loved Paul and me and was almost as much part of us as we were of one another. 'The gang will get Aristo and all those other bastards,' he said through the tears, 'you'll see if we don't.'

'Oh, God,' I whispered, 'oh, God, Marko, why wasn't I there?'

Chapter Thirty

The days passed and still Paul slept on. The doctor said that that kind of sleep was called a coma, and that we might have to take Paul to Athens. 'I've done what I can,' he told us sadly, 'but I am only a poor general practitioner. What he needs now is the help of a specialist . . . Do you understand what I am saying, Lella?'

'Doctor,' Grandmother answered, 'I am old and tired and I wish that I didn't understand anything.'

He put a hand on her arm. 'I know how much you've been through,' he said gently, 'but don't give up now.' He looked at me. 'How's Andi doing?' he asked.

'Not well, doctor. She won't sleep. I don't know what to do with her. All she wants to do is to sit up with Paul. She holds his hand and talks to him. All day long she never stops talking to him.'

The doctor rummaged in his bag and brought out a small bottle. 'Give her one of these half an hour before bedtime,' he said, 'they'll help her to sleep.' He went out but came back into the room as if he'd suddenly thought of something. They began talking in low voices and I caught the name 'Cassie' but then they went out into the hall. I left Paul and went to stand behind the door. If they were talking about my mother, then I wanted to know what they were saying.

'It's a trap,' the doctor was saying, 'she must not come down. It would be suicide. Everyone knows it's a trap.'

Grandmother said something I didn't catch but their voices rose a little. 'I know it's a trap to get her to come down,' she said. 'I know that's why they did it. I've sent word to her that she is not to come, but it's her child, doctor, and if she wants to come, nothing will stop her.'

'Listen, Lella,' the doctor pleaded, 'tell her that right now there is nothing that she can do. He won't even know she's there. And things might at last be improving. A little longer and she'll be able to walk the streets openly again. ELLAS is ready to take over. Markos now holds several towns and will soon be appointing a provisional government. Tell her to hold out till it happens.'

'Commander Markos might have the towns, but he is having to do a lot of fighting that he is neither used to, nor equipped for,' replied Grandmother, her voice once more strong and decisive. 'Right now it could go either way.'

'I won't argue with you, Lella. You know as much about the situation as I do, but whatever you do, tell her to stay away, convince her that there is nothing she can do for the boy at this stage.'

'You are a good doctor and a good man,' Grandmother replied, 'but don't forget she's a mother.'

The doctor drew a deep breath. 'Right,' he replied,

'right. Well, let's hope things will turn out all right.'

'Thank you, doctor. Let's hope so.'

I went back to sit by Paul. The news that Mother might come felt both good and bad. I didn't want her to come if it was dangerous but I did so want to see her. Perhaps, I thought, perhaps she'll sneak down one night when there isn't a moon. In the evening I took the pill that Grandmother gave me because I didn't want to argue with her about it. I'd planned to keep it under my tongue until she'd gone and then spit it out, but she wasn't in a hurry to leave and somehow I ended up swallowing it anyway.

I fought that pill all night, but it still worked. I slept more hours than I was awake and somewhere in between the two I heard the door open and someone came into the room and though it was very dark I knew that it could only be Mother. She moved softly across the floor as if afraid to wake us and when she reached Paul's bed she knelt down by it and buried her face in his hair and then her shoulders began to shake and then all of her shook and she was crying.

I drifted again but it can't have been for long because when I next opened my eyes Mother was still sitting by Paul, staring at him, her face distorted by pain and suffering.

'Mother,' I whispered. She looked up and put a finger to her lips. I managed to nod before a new wave of darkness swept over me. She'll come to me, I told myself hazily, when she's seen enough of Paul, she'll come to me.

But when I came round again she had gone and there

was a lot of screaming and shouting going on some-where and the sound of feet running down the stairs and scuffles seemed to break out in the yard which, as far as I could make out, then moved into the road. Soon afterwards the night was ripped open by gunfire.

I sat up with a start and swung my legs over the side of the bed. I wanted to go to the window but there was an ocean between it and me and by the time I had crossed it the night had once again grown quiet and still. I told myself that I must have been dreaming and my only thought was to get back to my bed but it was so far away and the floor was shifting and moving about under my feet making me feel as if I was on the high seas in a storm and that in turn made me dizzy and I knew that I wouldn't make it to my bed so I lay down beside Paul instead creeping close to him and putting my arms around him and tons of darkness came down on us and it was so heavy and dense that I had a job breathing and that is why I didn't notice that Paul wasn't.

Chapter Thirty-one

Paul was buried next to Great-Grandmother Hara in the little cemetery overlooking the bay, the one in which we'd played such a trick on the Warriors only months ago.

The whole school was given leave to follow the coffin. Dressed in their blue and white uniforms, the children walked with bowed heads and eyes red and swollen from crying. The villagers wept as the white coffin was carried out of the church and through the narrow alleys, past Anna's shop, the small, tatty, open-air cinema, the Secret Corner, our house, Ritzo's house, Notta the Herbpicker's house and lush lemon grove and then out on to the narrow, winding road, along the edge of the sea, and lastly up the gentle slope to the cemetery.

Grandmother and Aunt Dina walked beside us, Marko and me, holding our hands. Aunt Hara and Aunt Dina's boys followed close behind. Even cousin Aki was there. Aunt Hara had insisted on bringing him along in a cart belonging to the greengrocer. He'd been kind and thoughtful enough to grease the wheels but even so they grated terribly against the rough, stone-pitted road.

The service at the graveside was kept short. Afterwards the children were allowed to file past the open coffin one by one, each throwing a single flower on to the still form of my brother, before moving on. Paul looked for all the world as if he was just sleeping. He looked so peaceful: the long thick lashes shading his cheeks, the brown curls blowing ever so gently in the warm wind, the hint of a smile around his mouth. For a split second, in my mind's eye, I saw him as he used to look, asleep under the great eucalyptus trees at the bottom of our garden.

I so wanted to cry then, but the pain inside me was so big I felt nothing at all. That's how it had been ever since I'd woken up with him in my arms and they'd told me he was dead. And so I didn't cry. Not when the lid was at last put over him, shutting him off from me for ever, not when the coffin was lowered into the grave and the earth from the spade of Dimitri the orphan went thump, thump, as it piled on top of it, not when people pressed my hand and told me how sorry they were. Not even when Aristo touched me did I feel anything. Not until much later, when we were home again, without Paul – it would always be without Paul now – and Grandmother said very, very gently, 'Andi, my love, will you try to believe me if I tell you that time is the best healer for even the worst kind of bruises?'

'You mean that things don't hurt so much after a while,' I replied. I could feel my voice trembling but there was nothing I could do about that.

'Yes, my dove, that's what I mean.' She pulled me to her. 'You know that when you've grazed your knee a scab forms over the wound to protect it while it is healing. Then, in time, when it has done its job it falls off and though there will almost certainly be a scar left, the pain will have gone.'

I nodded because I could not speak. The tears, which I had not been able to let go before, now filled my eyes and rushed down my cheeks. 'Paul,' I whispered, 'Paul, Paul, Paul . . .'

Then I ran up to my room, tore down Aristo's kite, the 'Athenian', from the wall and turned it into matchsticks using only my hands.

Epilogue

I'd been with Father in Stockholm for almost three months before he could bring himself to tell me that Mother had been wounded in the shoot-out that followed after she'd come down from the hills to see Paul on the night that he died. It seems that though she was badly wounded she still managed to give Cyclops and his bloodhounds the slip. She had been making for the cave and might have reached it had she not heard their voices. She understood then that they must be close behind her so, not wanting to betray the location of the cave, she changed direction and picked the path to the *stani* instead. There she had managed to get inside the hut and on to Stammo's old iron bed, and under the pile of blankets that the old man's wife had left behind. That's where they found her shortly after dawn. But by then she was dead and it didn't matter any more what Old Cyclops did or said to her.

She was laid to rest beside Paul in the warm, thyme-scented soil of Greece in the little cemetery between the mountains and the sea, and it is good to know that nothing will ever separate them again.

Father and I often talk about them and of Greece and

our village, and when the pain gets too hard to bear any more, we cry, because although things will change some day they are bad now and we must stay here to live. Father says that I'll feel better once I start school here and get some friends of my own age instead of always being with him and his refugee friends. But I don't know.